CREEPY
CONDORS
OF
CALIFORNIA

Here's what readers from around the country are saying about Johnathan Rand's *AMERICAN CHILLERS:*

"Our whole class just finished reading 'Poisonous Pythons Paralyze Pennsylvania, and it was GREAT!"
-Trent J., age 11, Pennsylvania

"I finished reading "Dangerous Dolls of Delaware in just three days! It creeped me out!
-Brittany K., age 9, Ohio

"My teacher read GHOST IN THE GRAVEYARD to us. I loved it! I can't wait to read GHOST IN THE GRAND!"
-Nicholas H., age 8, Arizona

"My brother got in trouble for reading your book after he was supposed to go to bed. He says it's your fault, because your books are so good. But he's not mad at you or anything."
-Ariel C., age 10, South Carolina

"Thank you for coming to our school. I thought you would be scary, but you were really funny."
-Tyler D., age 10, Michigan

"American Chillers is my favorite series! Can you write them faster so I don't have to wait for the next one? Thank you."
-Alex W., age 8, Washington, D.C.

"I can't stop reading AMERICAN CHILLERS! I've read every one twice, and I'm going to read them again!"
-Emily T., age 12, Wisconsin

"Our whole class listened to CREEPY CAMPFIRE
CHILLERS with the lights out. It was really spooky!"
-Erin J., age 12, Georgia

"When you write a book about Oklahoma, write it about my
city. I've lived here all my life, and it's a freaky place."
-Justin P., age 11, Oklahoma

"When you came to our school, you said that all of your books
are true stories. I don't believe you, but I LOVE your books,
anyway!"
-Anthony H., age 11, Ohio

"I really liked NEW YORK NINJAS! I'm going to get all of
your books!"
-Chandler L., age 10, New York

"Every night I read your books in bed with a flashlight. You
write really creepy stories!"
-Skylar P., age 8, Michigan

"My teacher let me borrow INVISIBLE IGUANAS OF
ILLINOIS, and I just finished it! It was really, really great!"
-Greg R., age 11, Virginia

"I went to your website and saw your dogs. They are really
cute. Why don't you write a book about them?"
-Laura L., age 10, Arkansas

"DANGEROUS DOLLS OF DELAWARE was so scary that I
couldn't read it at night. Then I had a bad dream. That book
was super-freaky!"
-Sean F., age 9, Delaware

"I have every single book in the CHILLERS series, and I love them!"

     -Mike W., age 11, Michigan

"Your books rock!"

     -Darrell D ., age 10, Minnesota

"My friend let me borrow one of your books, and now I can't stop! So far, my favorite is WISCONSIN WEREWOLVES. That was a great book!"

     -Riley S., age 12, Oregon

"I read your books every single day. They're COOL!"

     -Katie M., age 12, Michigan

"I just found out that the #14 book is called CREEPY CONDORS OF CALIFORNIA. That's where I live! I can't wait for this book!"

     -Emilio H., age 10, California

"I have every single book that you've written, and I can't decide which one I love the most! Keep writing!"

     -Jenna S., age 9, Kentucky

"I love to read your books! My brother does, too!"

     -Joey B., age 12, Missouri

"I got IRON INSECTS INVADE INDIANA for my birthday, and it's AWESOME!"

     -Colin T., age 10, Indiana

#14: Creepy Condors of California

Johnathan Rand

An AudioCraft Publishing, Inc. book

This book is a work of fiction. Names, places, characters and incidents are used fictitiously, or are products of the author's very active imagination.

Graphics layout/design consultant: Scott Beard, Straits Area Printing
Honorary graphics consultant: Chuck Beard *(we miss you, Chuck)*
Editors: Sheri Kelley, Cindee Rocheleau

Book warehouse and storage facilities provided by Clarence and Dorienne's Storage, Car Rental & Shuttle Service, Topinabee Island, MI

Warehouse security provided by Salty, Abby and Lily Munster.

American Chillers #14: Creepy Condors of California

Paperback edition ISBN 1-893699-63-3
Hardcover edition ISBN 1-893699-64-1

Printed in USA

First Printing - June 2004

Creepy
Condors
of
California

Visit the official 'American Chillers' web
site at:

www.americanchillers.com

**Featuring excerpts from upcoming stories, interviews,
contests, official American Chillers wearables, and *more!*
Plus, join the FREE American Chillers fan club!**

1

"Okay, Class," Mrs. Kramer said to everyone on the bus, "while we're visiting the Los Angeles Zoo, I want everyone to be on their best behavior. And remember: we all stick together as a group. Does anyone have any questions?"

We all shook our heads.

"All right, then," Mrs. Kramer said as the bus driver opened the door. "Let's have fun!"

All of my classmates let out a cheer, and we leapt to our feet. Our teacher, Mrs. Kramer, had arranged for a field trip to the Los Angeles Zoo. I had never been there before, and I was really excited. I was so excited that I had a hard time falling asleep last night.

"Isn't this cool, Melanie?" my friend Sara asked as we stepped off the bus. The day was sunny and hot. Just about *every* day is sunny and hot in southern California, but I was glad to finally get out of that stuffy bus.

"I can't wait!" I exclaimed. "I've never been here before!"

There are a ton of animals to see at the zoo, but our class was more interested in a bird. Not just *any* bird, either. A California condor. We'd been studying them in class, and we learned that the California condor is the largest flying bird in North America. It has a wingspan of over *nine feet!* We learned a lot about them, and how they almost became extinct. They're still very rare. There are only about 200 of them left in the wild, and the rest are in zoos or research facilities. There are a few organizations that are working to help more California condors survive in the wild.

And today, we were going to see a real, live California condor, up close. Everyone in my class was really excited, including Mrs. Kramer.

We walked in a group to the zoo entrance. In minutes, we were inside. Mrs. Kramer was in front of us, and she stopped and turned.

"Does anyone know the name of the place where the birds are kept?" she asked. A few students raised their hands, but I was faster.

"Yes, Miss Doyle?"

"An aviary," I said. I knew this because my uncle used to work at an aviary, taking care of birds.

"Very good," Mrs. Kramer said. "Now, before we get to the aviary, I'd like to remind everyone to keep their hands outside of the cage. We don't want to disturb any of the birds."

We continued on, making our way past alligators, kangaroos, a big horn sheep . . . even a giraffe and an elephant! There sure are a lot of animals at the Los Angeles Zoo.

Finally, we came to the aviary, and when we saw the enormous condor perched on a large tree branch, we all gasped. The bird was *enormous* . . . bigger than I'd even imagined. It was almost all black. Most of the birds' head and neck were completely bare, except for a couple of feathers. Its head was a mix of different colors: blue, yellow, and red, mostly.

And not to be mean . . . but California condors aren't the prettiest birds you'll ever see. In fact, I thought that the one at the Los Angeles Zoo looked a bit scary.

But now, when I look back at that day and remember my field trip, I had no way of knowing that condors could not only be scary—they could be *horrifying.*

Terrifying.

Oh, the one at the zoo looked scary, all right, but my brother, Cameron and I would soon have an experience with California condors in the wild.

An experience that still gives me shivers to this day.

2

The school year ended, and, two weeks later, we started planning for our family vacation. Every summer we travel to northern California to Mt. Shasta to go camping in the foothills. Mt. Shasta is a long, long drive from Los Angeles.

But it's so much fun! The four of us—Mom, Dad, Cameron and I—camp in tents for a week. We go back to the same place every year. There are no houses, cars, or people. Just the four of us and the forest. We hike, fish, swim, and roast marshmallows at night. It's a blast!

But my favorite part is this:

In the foothills of Mt. Shasta, where we camp, I pan for gold in some of the mountain streams, and I've actually found real gold! Usually it's just tiny specks or flakes that aren't worth much money, but I don't care. I have a ton of fun panning for gold.

And this year was going to be even better, because I bought a metal detector with the money I'd made at my lemonade stand last summer. I was hoping that the metal detector would help me locate even bigger pieces of gold near some of the streams.

Wouldn't that be cool? To find a big gold nugget?

Cameron isn't really into gold panning. This year, he got a remote control airplane for his birthday, and he brought it with us on the trip so he could fly it around. But he had a problem the very moment he tried to get it off the ground.

"What's wrong with this thing?" he said to himself, turning the switch on and off. We had just finished unpacking the car and pitching the tents. Cameron and I had our own tent, and Mom and Dad had a tent right next to ours. I was testing out my metal detector, sweeping it over a can. The detector is sort of like a big golf club with a flat, round disc at the bottom. When you sweep the disc over metal, the machine makes a beeping sound.

I swept it over an unopened can of baked beans.

Beep—beep—beep.

"Cool!" I exclaimed.

"Yeah, well, *this* isn't so cool," Cameron said angrily.

"What's wrong?" I asked.

"This goofy plane won't work. The remote control works fine, but the plane won't turn on."

"Did you put in new batteries?" I asked.

A funny look came over Cameron's face. Then, with his free hand, he slapped his palm to his forehead.

"Batteries!" he cried. "I forgot to bring fresh batteries!"

"Bummer," I said.

"I can't believe I forgot them!" he exclaimed. "I had them right on my dresser."

"Double bummer," I said.

Cameron stuffed the remote control unit in his back pocket, carried the plane to the car, and he put it in the backseat.

"I guess that won't be much good for the rest of the week," he said with dismay.

"Want to go hunt for gold with me?" I asked.

"You never find much," he said, sitting on a stump. "It sounds boring."

"Hey, you never know," I said. "Now that I've got this metal detector, I might find a huge hunk of gold. I could get rich!"

Cameron shrugged. He's two years younger than me—I'm twelve, he's ten—and I kind of felt sorry for him. He was really planning on flying his airplane.

"Come on," I urged. "It'll be fun. You can pan for gold in the stream, and I'll use my metal detector on the riverbank. You never know . . . we just might find some gold."

Cameron stood up. "I guess it beats hanging around here," he said.

Mom and Dad were on the other side of their tent, preparing a place to make a fire.

"Mom," I said, "Can Cameron and I go look for gold?"

Mom stepped out from behind the tent. "Yeah," she replied, squinting in the bight sun. "Remember, just like last year: follow the stream so you don't get lost. Cameron, do you have your watch?"

Cameron held his arm up, displaying his wristwatch.

"Okay," Mom continued, looking at her own watch. "It's noon . . . be back here by four o'clock to get ready for dinner. And remember to take your canteens of water."

Four o'clock?!?! I thought. *That's four hours! We've got all afternoon to hunt for gold!*

I dug into my pack and found a small bottle that I use to carry gold in. Since I usually find tiny flecks of gold, I didn't really need to have anything bigger. And if we *were* lucky enough to find a bigger nugget, I could always carry it.

I stuffed the small bottle in the front pocket of my jeans, picked up my canteen, and clipped it to my belt loop. Then I picked up my pan that I use to look for gold. Cameron found his canteen and took a sip before he, too, clipped it to his belt loop. I handed him the pan.

"Ready?" I asked.

"Let's go," he said. "Bye Mom! Bye Dad! See you in a while!"

Mom and Dad waved, and Cameron and I turned and walked to the small stream that runs next to our camp site. It's only about as wide as a car and only a few feet deep.

And I didn't waste any time, either. I turned on my metal detector and immediately began sweeping it back and forth at the edge of the stream. Cameron knelt down on the riverbank and scooped up a pile of sand from the bottom of the stream, swishing it around until only the heaviest objects remained. That's how you pan for gold: if there's any gold in the pile of dirt in your pan, it will stay on the bottom. All of the lighter materials—sand and small pebbles—get washed away.

But we didn't have much luck. Slowly, we made our way farther and farther downstream. I continued with the metal detector, but I still hadn't found anything. Cameron was getting bored. He'd stopped panning altogether, and was just looking down into the stream as we walked.

"You're not going to find any gold that way," I said.

And it was at that exact moment his arm suddenly shot out. His eyes widened, and his jaw dropped.

"Oh my gosh!" he exclaimed. *"Look at that!"*

And when I saw what he was pointing at, I couldn't believe my eyes.

3

Me and my big mouth. I had just told my brother that he'd never find any gold without panning for it—but now we stood on the riverbank, looking at a shiny nugget of gold, gleaming back at us like a brilliant yellow eye from the bottom of the stream.

Cameron was so excited that he fell to his knees and thrust his arm into the water, soaking his shirt sleeve. He pulled his hand out of the water, stood up and opened his fist.

"Wow!" I shrieked. "I can't believe it!"

In his hand was a gold nugget, nearly the size of a pea. Now, you may not think that's very big, but let me tell you . . . a pea-sized gold nugget is considered huge.

"How much do you think it's worth?" Cameron asked excitedly.

"A lot!" I said. "Probably around twenty bucks!"

"Twenty bucks?!?!" he exclaimed. "And you said I wouldn't find any gold without using the pan!"

He shoved the gold nugget into his pocket, and we returned our gazes to the stream. If we found one nugget, there might be more.

"I can't believe you found that," I said. "I've never found a nugget that big."

"I'm going to find another one," Cameron said.

"As much as I'd like to find one, I think the chances aren't very good. That nugget was probably visible because the river has washed it downstream. Maybe we should head upstream and see if we could find where it came from."

"Not me," Cameron said, shaking his head. "If there's one nugget here, I'll bet there's more."

We searched and searched. While we walked, I kept the metal detector on, sweeping the disc-shaped foot a few inches above the ground. It never made a sound.

And we didn't see any more nuggets in the stream, either. Cameron went back to panning, but he found nothing.

Until—

"Wait a minute," he said, peering into the muddy pan. "I think I saw something."

I knelt down next to him. Cameron gently swished his fingers through the sand, sifting it away with the water.

"What did you see?" I asked.

"A shark," he remarked smartly.

"Yeah, right," I said, rolling my eyes.

"I saw something shiny. I did, really."

He sifted some more. Sure enough, we suddenly saw a shiny glint of light from the bottom of the pan—but when Cameron plucked it out with his thumb and forefinger, we discovered it was only a shiny piece of quartz. Quartz is a type of stone, and it can be really shiny, like glass.

"Bummer," I said with a sigh. Then I looked up and saw something that was so unexpected—so shocking—that the only thing I could do was stare.

4

I gasped.

"C . . . Cameron," I stammered quietly. "Move very slowly . . . and look up in that tree over there."

Cameron did as asked, and when he saw what I was looking at, his whole body shook.

"That's . . . that's—"

"That's a California condor!" I said, finishing his sentence.

Neither one of us could say anything more. Thirty feet away, sitting on a low branch, was a gigantic California condor . . . just like the one we'd seen at the Los Angeles Zoo.

Except for one thing.

The condor at the zoo had looked a little scary. Maybe because it was so big and strange looking.

The bird we were looking at in the tree, however, looked *angry*.

It looked *mean*.

That's crazy, I thought. *How can a condor be mean? It's just a bird.*

But Cameron sensed the same thing.

"Melanie," he whispered, *"take a look at its eyes. He looks like he's really mad at us or something."*

Cameron was right! The condor was looking at us like we had done something wrong . . . and maybe we had.

"Cameron," I said, "we have to get out of here. We might be near the bird's nest. If we are, the condor might feel threatened, even though we aren't going to try to hurt it."

All of a sudden, the enormous bird slowly spread its wings. It moved cautiously, watching us with those piercing, cold eyes. I felt a terrible chill.

Then the condor just sort of dipped forward. Its huge wings caught air, and the bird was suddenly swooping through the sky . . . away from us.

I let out a sigh of relief. Cameron did, too.

"That was so cool!" he said. "Wait until we tell Mom and Dad!"

"I wish we could have taken a picture," I said. "Not many people can say they've seen a real, live California condor in the wild."

Now we had *two* things to be excited about.

First, Cameron had found a gold nugget, which was really cool. Every once in a while he would take it out of his pocket and look at it.

And second, we saw a real, live, honest-to-goodness California condor.

"That thing really scared me for a minute," Cameron said.

"Me, too," I agreed. "He sure looked frightening. But we'll probably never see a California condor in the wild again."

Well, I was wrong about Cameron finding gold. I had told him that he wouldn't find any gold without panning, and I was wrong.

And I was wrong about the condor.

We would see it again . . . sooner than I'd ever imagined.

5

Cameron looked at his watch.

"Gosh, it's only twelve-thirty," he said. "We still have a lot of time left to hunt for gold."

And that's what we did. We continued along the stream, scouring the riverbank with the metal detector and panning in the stream. Cameron and I took turns, but we didn't have any luck. Panning for gold would be a hard way to make a living.

"Let's take a break," Cameron said, wiping the sweat from his forehead. He un-clipped his canteen of water from his belt loop and took a sip. I did the same, and we found a spot in the shade and sat down.

Cameron dug into his pocket and pulled out the gold nugget. He held it in his hand, inspecting it.

"Hard to believe they make coins out of this stuff," he said.

"And jewelry," I added. "Think about it, Cam. Over a hundred years ago, there might have been miners panning for gold in this very spot. When gold was discovered in California, people came from all over the world to find their fortune. Some people found gold nuggets the size of bowling balls."

Cameron let out a whistle. "That would be awesome," he said. "We'd be rich! I could buy a brand new car!"

"You can't even *drive*," I reminded him.

"Yeah, but it sure would be cool to be the only kid in school that had his own car. I could have Mom drive me to school and pick me up every day."

"Oh, I'm sure she'd *love* to do that," I said with a smirk.

"What would you do if you found a gold nugget that big?" he asked.

Good question.

"I guess I would save the money for college or something," I replied.

"Get out of here!" he said, recoiling. "You mean to tell me that you wouldn't spend *any* of it?!?!"

"Well, I might. I might buy some clothes and some compact discs."

"I'd buy a sports car," Cameron said, making noises like a car engine. "One that goes super-fast. *That's* what *I* would buy."

That's my brother for you.

"Well, we aren't going to find any gold sitting here in the shade," I said. "Come on."

We stood. I picked up my metal detector and began sweeping it just above the ground. Cameron walked to the edge of the stream and began dipping the pan into the water.

"Hey! I caught a fish in the pan!" he exclaimed.

I walked to where he was kneeling and bent over.

Sure enough, a small fish was darting around in the pan.

"Maybe we could take it back to Mom and Dad and tell them that we caught dinner," I said with a smirk. Cameron laughed, tilting the pan sideways to let the fish escape.

But then he stopped laughing. He was staring down into the water with a horrified look upon his face.

"What is it?" I asked, thinking that maybe he saw a snake. Cameron is terrified of snakes.

I looked down into the stream, but I didn't see anything that would cause Cameron to freak out.

Then, as I continued looking, I realized that it wasn't something *in* the water that Cameron was looking at.

It was a *reflection* in the water.

Something big.

And dark.

Something from above was coming at us, and fast.

A shadow suddenly fell over us, and I turned and looked up.

A California condor.

He was coming right at us, claws bared, beak wide.

And those *eyes*.

Cold, lifeless eyes glared at us.

Angry eyes that burned with fury.

When we studied California condors in school, we learned that they don't attack people. Period.

But this condor *was* attacking, and I knew already there was no way we could escape the terrible beast as it hurled toward us at lightning speed. The only thing I could do was close my eyes . . . and scream.

6

All of a sudden, I was sent flying sideways, tumbling to the ground. I almost fell into the stream, but I rolled backwards just in time.

Not two feet away, the enormous condor clenched its claws, but grabbed nothing. Cameron, too, had rolled to the side, away from the attacking bird.

The condor, its claws empty, swept upward. I could feel the movement of air generated by the bird's massive wings.

And then I figured out why the condor hadn't been able to grab me. At the very last possible moment, Cameron had pushed me. He pushed me out of the path of the attacking bird, and then he leapt out of the way himself.

Above us, the condor continued its ascent, rising above the trees, floating on its huge wings.

"You . . . you saved me!" I stammered.

"Yeah, but let's not talk about that now!" Cameron shouted, kneeling in the long grass and looking up at the bird. "That thing might come after us again!"

And that's exactly what the bird did. The condor suddenly rolled sideways, arcing around and heading right for us!

"Run!" I shouted, grabbing my metal detector and the pan. Cameron and I leapt to our feet and began running like mad. I didn't even turn to see where the condor was. I knew that it was coming after us, and if I chanced a glance over my shoulder, I might trip and fall.

Then it would be all over.

Dozens of questions buzzed in my head as I ran. *Why is it attacking us? Why is it so big? Where did it come from?*

Condors are supposed to be scavengers, not dangerous predators.

Yet, that is exactly what the condor was doing: attacking. It was a predator . . . and we were the prey!

A branch smacked my cheek and I winced in pain, but I didn't slow down. I didn't dare!

Cameron was right in front of me, and he darted around a huge pine tree. I followed . . . and just in the nick of time. The condor shot past the tree, missing me by mere inches. Once again it swooped up, only this time it disappeared into the trees.

"What is that thing?!?!" Cameron gasped, his back pressed against the tree trunk.

"It's a California condor," I gasped back.

"I know *that*," Cameron replied. "But why is it attacking?"

I shook my head. "You've got me," I said, still trying to catch my breath. I had been running hard, and my lungs hurt. My face was covered with a thin film of sweat. I used my metal detector as a cane, leaning forward on it with one hand, and carrying the silver pan in the other.

"Let's stay here a minute," Cameron said. "This tree is pretty big. If that thing comes after us again, we can run around to the other side of the trunk."

That sounded like a good idea. We were probably safer near the tree than we would be running through the forest.

We waited, our heads turned up, eyes scanning the trees and the intermittent splotches of blue sky. There was no sign of the bird.

"Maybe he's gone," Cameron said, still scanning the sky.

"We've got to get back to camp and tell Mom and Dad," I said. "That thing is really dangerous."

Cameron agreed, and we warily began walking back.

But not for long. We stopped walking after only a minute or two.

"I think we go that way," Cameron said, pointing.

"I thought we came from that direction," I replied, pointing in an entirely different direction. "All we have to do is find the stream and follow it back to camp. I think it's over there."

"No, it looks more familiar over that way," Cameron insisted, and he began walking. Reluctantly, I followed him. Both of us kept glancing nervously up into the sky, up at tree branches, looking for any sign of the condor.

Finally, after walking for a few minutes, Cameron stopped. He looked around.

"This doesn't look familiar at all," he admitted.

He was right, and I began to realize that we were in a lot of trouble . . . for two reasons.

Reason one: we were lost, and I knew it.

Reason two: flapping wings. We could hear the sound of flapping wings through the trees, coming closer and closer with every passing second.

The condor had returned.

7

"It's coming!" I screamed. "It's coming back!"

Our heads darted frantically, searching for the bird, ready to run, to dive out of the way, ready to do whatever we would need to do to escape.

"Where is it?!?!" Cameron exclaimed. "Where is he coming from?!?!"

Suddenly, I caught a glimpse through the branches. I gasped . . . and then breathed a heavy sigh of relief. Above us, two crows flew past.

"Whew," Cameron said, breathing his own sigh of relief. "I thought the condor had come back."

"Me, too," I said, leaning on my metal detector.

We said nothing for a few moments. Then, I spoke.

"Well, we can do one of two things. We can stay here and wait for someone to come looking for us, or we can keep going and try to find the stream."

Cameron looked at his watch. "It's only twelve forty-five," he said. "We've only been gone forty-five minutes. Mom and Dad won't come looking for us until we don't show up at camp at four o'clock. I say we keep moving. That stream has got to be around here somewhere."

"I don't know," I said. "I've always read that if you're lost, it's best to stay in one place and stay calm."

"It's hard to stay calm when you have a giant canary trying to eat you," Cameron muttered.

Good point.

"All right," I said. "Let's see if we can find the stream."

And so, we started out again. I carried the metal detector, and I handed the pan to Cameron for him to carry.

But no matter where I looked, nothing appeared familiar. We would stop every few minutes and listen for the babble of water that would tell us that we were near the stream, but we didn't hear anything except the normal sounds of the forest.

At least we didn't see any sign of the condor, which was a relief. Maybe he had flown off to somewhere else.

I was becoming more and more frustrated, and so was Cameron. The day was hot, I was tired, and we still hadn't found the stream. I began to worry that we might never get out of the forest. And even if Mom and Dad came looking for us, they might not find us before nightfall.

And that *really* scared me. I did *not* want to be out in the woods after dark.

"Let's rest for a few minutes," I said. "It's really hot, and I need a drink of water."

We walked to a large tree and stood in the shade. A light breeze cooled my skin.

"This is better," I said, leaning the metal detector against the tree trunk. Cameron set the pan on the ground and un-clipped his canteen from his belt loop. I sat down and reached for my own canteen . . . not even realizing what was perched on a branch right above us.

I unscrewed the cap on my canteen, lifted it to my lips, closed my eyes, and tilted my head back. The water wasn't very cold, but it was still very refreshing. I was careful to only drink a little bit. After all, if we really *were* lost, we would have to conserve all of the water we had.

I opened my eyes . . . and nearly choked on my last gulp of water.

The condor was sitting on a branch right above us!

I was too afraid to move.

"Cameron!" I hissed quietly, still holding the canteen near my lips.

"What?" he replied, completely unaware of the bird perched above.

"Don't . . . move . . . an . . . inch," I said, slowly and quietly.

"Why?" he asked.

"Look . . . up . . . slowly," I said.

I heard Cameron gasp, and I knew that he'd spotted the condor.

"He's not looking down," I whispered. *"Maybe he hasn't spotted us."*

My heart was beating faster and faster. What would the condor do if he spotted us? Would he attack again?

As I gazed up at the bird, I realized again that it was somehow different than the California condors that I'd seen in pictures, and certainly different from the one I'd seen at the zoo back home in Los Angeles. California condors are big . . .but this one was *huge*.

And its claws . . . .

There was something very different about its claws, but I just couldn't figure out what it was. The claws were different than a normal condor's claws, but I just couldn't put my finger on it.

Out of the corner of my eye, I caught a flicker of movement in the sky. Cameron and I both let out a gasp as yet *another* condor came into view! It swooped over the trees, circled once, and soared down, landing on the branch right next to the condor above us!

My fear grew. We had been able to get away from one condor . . . but what would happen if both condors attacked us at the same time?

I couldn't bear to even *think* about it.

The two condors didn't seem to be paying attention to one another. They just sat silently, without moving, staring off into the distance. Once every few seconds, one of them would cock its head to the side, but other than that, they didn't move.

Finally, one of the giant birds slowly spread its wings. They were gigantic! The condor looked more like a plane than a bird!

It dipped forward and took flight, catching wind and soaring off and up into the sky. In seconds, it had vanished, leaving the single condor sitting alone on the branch above us.

Please fly away, I thought. *Oh, please, Mr. Condor. Please fly away . . . please fly—*

Without warning, the bird spread its wings, stretching them out.

Yes! I thought. *He's going to fly off! He's going away!*

But suddenly, the condor turned its head.

It looked right down at us, made a strange grunting sound . . . and attacked!

Once again, we were forced to defend ourselves from the ravaging bird. There was no time to wonder why, no time to wonder just what was happening. We had to get away from the horrific creature, and *fast.*

I rolled to the right, and Cameron rolled to the left. Pine needles and twigs dug into my elbows. Both of us scrambled behind the tree trunk. The condor swooped down, claws extended, but he missed. The bird rose up and circled preparing for his next attack.

"Get out of here!" Cameron shouted. *"Go home! Leave us alone!"*

If the condor could understand English, he didn't pay any attention. Again, it swooped down at us, and we ran around to the other side of the tree to get away from it. Only this time, the bird didn't fly away. It landed on the ground, right in front of us! Its wings were extended, and the bird stood upright on its legs, facing us.

And when I say it was *huge,* I mean it was *enormous!* Standing up on its legs like it was, the condor was taller than Cameron and me!

The bird made a hop in our direction, and I screamed. Cameron leapt back, but not before he had grabbed the metal detector that was still leaning against the tree.

"Stay back!" he warned, holding out the metal detector like a sword. I ran behind him as the bird came closer and closer.

"I'm warning you!" Cameron shouted, waving the metal detector. "I'll use this thing! I really will!"

The bird began flapping its wings, but it didn't fly off. Cameron lunged forward with the metal detector, and a strange thing happened:

The metal detector started beeping! Whenever the detector got close to the bird, it made a beeping sound, like it was near metal!

The condor kept coming, and Cameron refused to back down, using the metal detector to keep the bird back. I stayed behind Cameron, unsure of what to do.

I wanted to run, but I couldn't leave my brother to fend for himself.

And besides . . . so far, he was succeeding in keeping the condor away.

Then the bird took a single hop back. Flapping its wings, it took to the air—and came right for us.

Cameron stood his ground, and he swung the metal detector just as the bird made its assault. The detector beeped madly as it made contact with the condor.

"Get . . . away!" Cameron shouted as he swung.

Suddenly, the bird stopped flapping its wings. It collapsed without warning and fell to the ground.

It made no movement, no sounds.

The condor was dead.

10

Two emotions swelled up inside me.

First: relief. We had stopped the giant condor from attacking, and we'd probably saved our lives.

But secondly, I was horrified. We'd actually *killed* a California condor, which was bound to land us in big trouble. We might even go to jail!

"Oh my gosh!" Cameron exclaimed. He was horrified. "I didn't mean to kill it! I just wanted him to go away and leave us alone!"

We stared at the bird in silence. Even at the Los Angeles Zoo, we hadn't been able to get this close to a condor. Now, one was at our feet, and we were mere *inches* from it.

Except for one big difference:

The condor at our feet was dead.

And still, I knew there was something really different about this condor. Sure, its feathers were black, like most condors. Its head was blue and pink and red and orange.

But its *eyes* . . . .

They were so black, so shiny, that they didn't even look real.

I knelt down, careful not to touch the bird. I pointed to the bird's claws.

"Look," I urged Cameron. He knelt down beside me.

"What?" he asked.

"Look at its claws," I said. "They're different than a normal condors' claws."

"They look fine to me," Cameron said.

"No, they're different. I don't know *how* they're different, but they are. I remember reading something about their claws in school."

"It looks like a big, dead bird, that's all," Cameron said with a shrug.

"Wait a minute," I said. "Hand me the metal detector."

Cameron had dropped the metal detector when the bird had fallen, and now he picked it up and handed it to me.

I stood up, sweeping the round disc over the bird. Immediately, the detector began beeping.

"Why is it doing that?" Cameron asked.

"It shouldn't be doing anything," I replied. "This thing is only supposed to beep when it's near metal."

I continued sweeping the detector over the bird. Whenever I drew the unit away from the condor, it stopped beeping.

"That's weird," Cameron said.

"It's *really* weird," I said. "It shouldn't do that."

"Maybe it's broken," Cameron suggested.

"No," I said, shaking my head. "I don't think so."

I lowered the disc to the condor and gave it several pokes . . . and an amazing thing happened. What we saw made Cameron and I both gasp in astonishment.

11

A part of the bird fell off!

At first, I thought it was a clump of feathers, and it was—sort of.

But it looked too uniform . . . too *perfect*. I used the disc of the metal detector and pushed it away, revealing wires and electrical parts.

"No way!" Cameron exclaimed.

"It's . . . it's—" I stammered.

"It's mechanical!" Cameron said, finishing my sentence.

"That's impossible!" I exclaimed, setting down the metal detector and kneeling once again.

"And look!" Cameron said, dropping down next to me. He reached out and pulled at a few wires. An ordinary battery fell out. "It's battery powered! And that little box right there is a receiver! My airplane has one!"

"You mean that this thing is remote controlled?" I asked.

Cameron nodded. "Just like my airplane," he replied.

"But by who?" I asked. "Where?" There's nobody around for miles."

"I don't know," Cameron said. "But now we know why the metal detector kept beeping whenever the disc was close to the condor."

"Do you think we broke the bird?" I asked.

"I don't think so," Cameron said. "I think I just knocked the battery loose. If I put it back into place, the bird will probably start flapping like crazy. He might even try to attack us."

Which was really weird. It was weird that a condor would attack a human being in the first place, but it was even weirder to discover that the very same condor wasn't even real.

"Well, don't put the battery back in," I said. "I don't want that thing coming to life again."

"I'll bet there's a power switch somewhere," Cameron said, and he touched the bird's wing. "Geez . . . they even feel like feathers . . . sort of."

I reached out and felt the feathers. They were soft, but they also had a different texture. Have you ever felt fake hair? That's kind of what it felt like.

"Help me look," Cameron said. "Let's see if we can find a switch or a button that will turn the bird on and off."

Cameron plunged his fingers into the feathers, feeling around the condor's legs. I lifted up the wing, which wasn't easy. It was heavy!

But beneath the wing, right near the body, was a space where there were no feathers. It was a small space, about the size of the palm of my hand. Sure enough, right in the middle of it was an on/off button.

"There it is!" I said, and Cameron reached out and pressed the button to the *off* position.

"That should do it," he said, and he placed the battery back into place.

The bird didn't move.

"How do we know we didn't break it?" I asked.

"We'll have to turn it on," Cameron said.

"No way," I said, shaking my head defiantly.

Cameron was peering at the wires and at the small receiver nestled within the electrical components.

Suddenly, his eyes lit up.

"That's it!" he said excitedly. "I bet it'll work!"

"What?" I asked. "What will work?"

He reached into his back pocket. "Look what I've got!" he exclaimed.

And when he showed me what he had in his hand, I knew what his idea was.

Even better . . . it was a good idea, that just *might* work.

12

In Cameron's hand was the remote control for his airplane! He had stuffed it in his pocket when he put the airplane back into the car!

"You think . . . you think you can control the condor with that thing?" I asked.

"Yeah!" Cameron said. "I think I can! All we have to do is make sure that this remote control and the receiver in the bird are on the same frequency."

He reached over and inspected the receiver closer. "There's a switch right there," he said.

"But how will you know if it's the right frequency?" I asked.

"Well, the bird won't work unless the remote control and the receiver in the condor are on the same frequency. My remote control has only one frequency, so I can't change it. But the receiver in the condor looks like it has a few frequencies to choose from."

Sometimes my brother can be a real pain, but he's always been really smart . . . and right now, I was really glad.

"Okay," I said. "Suppose we get the thing working. Then what? We're still lost."

"First things first," Cameron said. "Help me stand this thing up."

"What about that cover thing?" I asked. On the ground was a small object, made of soft plastic and covered with feathers. It was the cover for the battery and receiver compartment.

"We'll leave it off, just in case I need to change the frequency," he said. "Come on."

It took both of us to stand the condor up. And it was hard to get the thing to balance, too. After all, it was taller than we were. Plus, I think it weighed a hundred pounds!

"There," Cameron said. "Now, let's turn the thing on."

Cameron reached under the bird's wing and pressed the on/off button.

"Okay," he continued, "let's see if we can get this bird in the air. Stand back."

We both took a few steps back. I sure didn't want to be anywhere near that thing if it went out of control!

Cameron tried several knobs on his remote control, but he didn't have any luck.

"Let's try another frequency," he said, and he stepped up to the massive bird, fiddled with a small knob next to the battery compartment, then stepped away again.

Still, there was no movement from the bird.

"Maybe we broke it, after all," I said.

"No, no," Cameron said. "This will work. It has to."

But no matter what frequency he tried, the condor showed no movement.

Suddenly Cameron looked down at the remote control in his hand. A frustrated look came over his face.

"Of course!" he said. "How can I be so goofy?!?! The remote control is turned off!"

With a flick of his finger he turned the remote control on . . . and that's when things got *really* interesting.

13

The moment Cameron turned on the power to the remote control, the condor sprang to life! It surprised both of us so much that we jumped back a few steps.

The condor began walking around! It was a bit frightening, but it was also kind of cool at the same time.

Cameron was frantically messing around with the controls. It took him a minute, but he was finally able to control the bird and make it stop.

"Do you think you can make it fly?" I asked.

"We won't know unless we try," he replied. "Here goes nothing."

And with a flick of his wrist, he turned a knob. Suddenly, the condor started flapping its wings! It didn't fly, but it sure made a commotion.

"So far, so good," Cameron said. "A little bit more—"

All at once the condor was in the air . . . but the problem was, he was coming right at us!

"Watch out! Watch out!" I screamed, and both of us had to duck so the flying creature didn't hit us.

"Can't you get control of that thing?!?!" I asked.

"I'm trying! I'm trying!" Cameron answered. "It works kind of like my airplane, but not exactly. This is hard!"

"Well, you'd better figure it out quick," I said. "It's headed right for that tree!"

"I told you! I'm trying! It's just . . . just . . . *there!*"

Suddenly, the condor swung to the left . . . and just in time, too. Its wings even clipped some of the tree branches.

"That was close," Cameron said, "but I think I've got it. Watch."

I continued gazing up at the flying condor. It wasn't flapping its wings anymore, but rather, its wings were outstretched all the way, and the bird was literally riding air currents.

"Now I'll make it dip," Cameron said. Instantly, the condor swooped lower. Then it rose back up into the sky.

"You're doing it!" I exclaimed

"Now I'll bring it back right over us," Cameron said, adjusting the knobs on the remote control. The bird took a sharp dive and flew right over our heads.

"This is cool!" Cameron said. "Watch . . . I think I can even control its claws."

Sure enough, I could see the condor's claws clenching and unclenching.

"Wait until my friends at school see this!" Cameron exclaimed. "They're going to freak!"

"You forgot that we're still lost," I said.

"Yeah, but we'll find our way out of here. And you know what? I bet we could really scare Mom and Dad with this thing!"

I laughed out loud. In my mind, I could see the condor swooping through the camp, and Mom and Dad running for cover.

But then, of course, we'd get into a lot of trouble.

"Can you land that thing?" I asked.

"Probably," Cameron replied. "But it's a lot different than flying my airplane."

He sure was having a lot of fun. I was too, I guess. It really was cool watching the huge bird fly through the sky. It was even cooler knowing that Cameron was controlling the bird by remote control. In fact, we were so engrossed in watching the bird in flight that we forgot one important thing.

We had seen not just *one* condor . . . but *two*.

Somewhere, there was another one of these condors.

One we had no control over.

And it was about to return.

14

I spotted the bird first.

"Cameron!" I shrieked. *"Look!"*

High in the sky, another condor was racing toward us. There was no mistake about it: we were targets.

"Run!" Cameron shouted, holding out the remote control in front of him. He was trying to control the condor while he ran.

As for me, I just wanted to get somewhere safe as quick as possible. Sure, there wasn't really any place to hide, but if we could make it to a tree—

Suddenly, I was sent sprawling to the ground. The condor had struck me! I could hear its flapping wings above my head. I rolled on the ground, and I didn't stop until I hit something solid.

"Melanie!" I heard Cameron shout. "Are you all right?!?!"

"Yes!" I shouted back. "Where did the condor go?!?!"

"He flew up, but now he's coming back around! Get behind that tree!"

I leapt to my feet and darted behind the tree, just as Cameron ordered, not even taking the time to see where the attacking condor was. And it was a good thing, too . . . because the hideous flying beast was making another attack at that very moment. I managed to make it behind the tree just in time.

"Stay where you are!" I heard Cameron shout. Although I couldn't see where he was through the trees and branches, I knew my brother wasn't far away.

The condor that had attacked remained circling above the tree that I was hiding beneath. But then *another* condor showed up . . . and began attacking the condor that had attacked *me!*

Then I figured it out. Cameron was doing it! He was controlling the condor with remote control, and he was attacking the other bird with it!

"It's working!" I shouted. "Where are you?!?!"

"I'm over here!" Cameron shouted. "But don't move from that tree yet! I don't know what's going to happen!"

"Whatever you're doing, you're doing great!" I cheered.

And he was. Cameron was making his condor dive-bomb the other condor. The other bird didn't seem to know what to do. It didn't fight back, and every time Cameron's condor swooped down, the bird dove to the side. Finally, it flew off and vanished. Cameron kept his condor circling in the air.

"Okay," he said. "I think we're safe now."

I came out from behind the tree. Instantly, I saw Cameron. He had done the same thing as I had: hidden on the other side of a large tree trunk.

We walked to a clearing, with Cameron still holding out his remote control, gazing up at the soaring condor.

"Now," he said, "let's see if we can bring her down for a landing."

In just the few minutes of working with the remote control, he'd gotten pretty good at steering the bird. With a few adjustments, the bird was swooping down toward us. But as he tried to bring the condor down for a landing, it became clumsy and jerky.

"Careful," I said, as the bird almost clipped a tree.

"Hey, I'm just learning how to control this thing," Cameron protested. "Give me a break."

And he was doing okay, right up to the point when he tried to get the condor to extend its legs in time to land on the ground. Cameron wasn't quick enough with the controls, and the bird slowed, slowed more, and then plunged forward, beak first, into the ground.

"Ouch," I said.

"Hey, nobody's perfect," Cameron sneered.

We walked up to the fallen condor. Except for some dust on its head and some grass in its feathers, the mechanical bird appeared to be fine.

But I finally noticed what was different about the bird's claws.

"Cameron!" I suddenly shrieked. *"Look at the condor's claws!"*

"Yeah?" he said. "What about them?"

"They're opposable!"

"What?" he said. "What does 'opposable' mean?"

"It means that it has a toe that faces *backward!* Real condors *don't* have opposable toes! That means that they can't grasp anything. They can't pick anything up and carry it off . . . but this mechanical condor can!"

"So?" Cameron remarked. "Big deal."

"It *is* a big deal," I said. "It's a *huge* deal. It means we might be able to find our way back to the stream!"

Cameron looked really confused. "How in the world are claws going to help us find the stream?"

But when I told him my idea, his jaw dropped.

"Melanie!" He exclaimed. *"You're a genius! That really might work!"*

Well, it *would* work.

It would work *too* well.

And this is where something happened that changed the entire day . . . and our lives . . . forever.

15

Here was my plan:

Being that the condor was able to pick things up, I thought that the condor could pick *me* up. Cameron could guide the bird—and me—up into the air, just high enough to that I would be able to see the stream. I would yell down to him, and he could lower me back to earth.

"You're not afraid?" Cameron asked.

"Of course I'm afraid," I said. "But I'm more afraid of being lost in the woods. Especially at night."

Cameron looked at his watch. "It's fifteen minutes after one. We still have almost three hours before Mom and Dad will come looking for us. We might as well give your idea a try. But what if the bird isn't strong enough to carry you?"

"We won't know until we try," I said. "Come on. We're wasting time just standing here."

I un-clipped my canteen, unscrewed the lid, and took a sip. I replaced the lid and set the canteen next to the metal detector and the pan. The canteen of water wasn't *that* heavy, but it would be extra weight that might make it harder for the condor to pick me up.

The two of us righted the bird and stood it up straight. Standing there in the grass, motionless as it was, it reminded me of a stuffed bird, the kind that you see in big lodges or at hunting clubs. The bird didn't look alive.

Which, of course, it wasn't.

With Cameron at the remote control, the bird was aloft in no time at all.

"Okay," Cameron said, guiding the bird as it circled above our heads. "How do you want to do this?"

"Bring it straight down over my head," I said. "I'll reach my hands up like this—" I raised my arms straight up. "This way, not only can the condor get a good grip around my arms, but I'll be able to hold onto its legs with my hands, just in case you screw up and it loses its grip."

"I'm not going to screw up!" he protested loudly.

"Good," I said. "I hope not. Now . . . lower the bird down."

As I looked up, hands in the air, the condor beat its wings, coming straight down at me. Its legs were extended and its claws were apart.

"Remember," I said, "to listen close. When you hear me shout that I want down, bring me down."

"Got it," Cameron said with a nod. "You ready?"

I nodded.

Cameron made some adjustments with the remote control, and the condor lowered even more. I could feel the wind generated by its powerful, flapping wings.

Then I was grasping the mechanical birds' legs, and I felt its claws snugly settling around my forearms.

"Still ready?" Cameron said.

"Yep," I replied, but I wasn't really sure. After all, I was about to be lifted high into the air. If something went wrong . . . .

No, I told myself. *Nothing is going to go wrong. This is the only way. If we want to find the stream and get out of here, this is what we're going to have to do. Nothing will go wrong.*

I was seconds away from being lifted higher than the treetops.

I was also seconds away . . . from disaster.

16

"Okay . . . here we go."

Cameron spoke carefully as he held the remote control out in front of him. I could feel the condor's wings beating harder, but so far, I hadn't budged an inch. I was still on the ground.

"Come on, come on," Cameron urged, working with the remote control. I could feel the tight grip of the condor's claws clasping my forearms, and I could even feel myself being pulled upward. But so far, my feet hadn't left the ground.

In an instant, that all changed.

Suddenly, my feet *did* leave the ground, and I found myself being drawn upward really fast. In a second, I was ten feet off the ground.

"Slow down!" I shouted.

"Hang on, hang on!" Cameron shouted as he goofed around with the remote control.

The bird began to slow, but I was still really afraid. By now, I was almost at treetop level. I didn't think I would rise up so quickly.

And suddenly, I was above the trees. My fear faded, and I knew I was going to be okay. It was so cool! I could see for miles and miles! Beneath me was a carpet of trees. In the distance, I could see the snowy white cap of Mt. Shasta. Thankfully, I didn't see any other condors.

But the best part of all:

The stream!

Not far away, I could see the stream winding through the forest!

"I can see it!" I shouted down to Cameron. "I can see the stream!"

I was really proud of myself. My plan had worked! I knew that if the condor could lift me high enough, I'd be able to find the stream. Now that we knew which direction it was, we'd be able to find it. We weren't lost anymore.

"Okay!" I shouted. "You can bring me down now!"

"Okay!" Cameron's voice echoed through the trees.

But nothing happened. I remained where I was, suspended in the air, clinging tightly to the mechanical bird above my head.

"Hey!" I shouted. "I said I saw the stream! You can bring me down now!"

"I'm . . . I'm trying!" Cameron shouted.

"What's the matter?!?!" I shouted back.

"It's not doing anything!" Cameron replied. I looked down and I could see the terror in his face. "I'm trying to control the bird," he continued, "but it isn't responding to the remote control!"

I gripped the bird's legs even tighter. If Cameron didn't have control of the condor, it might let go of me at any minute!

Suddenly, the condor began to circle around, and a wave of relief washed over me.

Whew, I thought. *He got it working.*

But in the next moment, I realized something was very wrong.

"Cameron! What are you doing?!?!" I shouted as the condor caught an air current and rose even higher.

"Nothing!" Cameron shouted back, and I could hear the fear in his voice. Whatever the condor was doing, it was doing it on its own.

"Cameron!" I shouted again.

"It won't respond!" Cameron shrieked, only this time, his voice was distant, farther away. "I can't control it!"

There was nothing I could do except hang on and hope for the best. I certainly wasn't going to struggle, because that might make the condor release me.

Once in a while, when I really think that things are going good, I find out how wrong I am.

Not this time.

This time, I was sure that something awful was going to happen.

And I was *right*.

17

I have never been so completely terrified in my entire life. I'm not afraid of heights, and I'm not even afraid of flying. We have relatives in Michigan, and we've flown there several times in airplanes. It's kind of fun.

But this was an entirely different kind of flying, as you can imagine!

I looked down, and I could no longer see Cameron. The condor carried me high in the sky, over the stream where we'd been panning for gold. I tried to see our camping spot, but the trees were too thick.

Then I had another terrible thought.

The condor was battery powered. What if the batteries died while I was being carried high in the sky? Would the bird simply slow and glide down to earth, or would it drop like a rock . . . carrying me with it?

I wished I'd never left the ground. Being lost in the forest was a lot better than being carted off by a giant, mechanical bird!

I turned my head around, and I spotted Cameron. He was just a little speck on the ground, running through a field, trying to follow me.

"Cameron!" I shrieked as loud as I could. *"Do something! Do anything!"*

I don't know if he heard me or not. If he did, he didn't reply, or, at least, I didn't hear anything from him.

Higher and higher the condor soared, billowed by the strong air currents. Was it taking me somewhere? Or was it just flying, circling around, out of control?

By now, even the trees below me looked like tiny dots . . . and that's when the condor changed its course.

We had been circling around, rising higher and higher. All of a sudden the condor turned slightly, and began to head into the distance . . . straight toward Mt. Shasta!

Is that where it's taking me? I wondered. *To Mt. Shasta? Why?*

I'd find out soon enough. Mt. Shasta wasn't very far away, and at the speed we were traveling, it wasn't going to take us long to get there.

On and on we flew, and Mt. Shasta grew. I could make out jutting cliffs and snowy peaks. That's where we were headed, all right.

But it was too late when I realized what was happening. The condor was flying, soaring with its wings spread, traveling very, very fast.

But it was out of control. There was no place for the bird to land anywhere . . . just solid rock walls.

"Stop!" I shouted. I knew it wouldn't do any good, but shouting felt better than doing *nothing!*

The condor continued its course, and I realized that it was all over. In seconds, we would slam into the side of the mountain.

"Nooooooo!" I shrieked. *"Nooooooo!"*

18

The rock wall loomed in front of me, closer and closer by the second. I knew that there was no place for the bird to land, and there was nothing I could do but wait to slam into the side of the mountain.

But it didn't happen. Just when I had lost all hope, and I was certain we were about to hit the side of Mt. Shasta, the condor made a quick turn. A large cave on the other side of a cliff came into view! The condor turned once again, dove down . . . *and flew into the tunnel!*

Daylight vanished, and I was suddenly plunged into darkness. Which was a different type of fear altogether. Not being able to see where we were going was *really* scary, and I hoped that we didn't hit a wall or anything.

The only thing I could hear was the rush of wind in my ears and the condor's enormous wings above me.

How long was this going to go on? Where was the mechanical bird taking me?

I was horrified. I wanted to be back in the forest with Cameron. I didn't care if we were lost or not. *Anything* was better than this.

Deeper and deeper we went into the tunnel. My eyes were open, but it didn't matter. There was absolutely nothing to see but darkness.

And then there *was* something to see.

Up ahead.

A tiny speck of light. Not a bright light like the sun or anything, but a gray, misty light. As we drew nearer, the light grew a little brighter. It looked like the cave we were traveling through was going to open into a big cavern.

Which was pretty amazing, when you think about it. I was being carried *inside* Mt. Shasta! I never knew that something like this would be possible.

But if I was amazed by what was happening, I was even more amazed by the spectacle that I was now seeing below me.

19

The mouth of the tunnel suddenly opened up into an enormous cavern. And when I say *enormous,* I mean *enormous!*

But what was even more incredible was what I was seeing.

Ahead of me, in the air, were several more condors, circling and soaring! One of the condors was carrying a person in its claws, just like I was being carried! Far off, on the other side of the cavern, was a gigantic HOLLYWOOD sign, just like the real sign sitting on the side of a hill in the city of Hollywood. Each letter is gigantic . . . bigger than most houses.

Behind the giant letters, searchlights sent arrows of light upwards. The beams swept back and forth.

And far below me—

A city!

Well, sort of. I could see houses and cars. There were people running all over. Sirens wailed, and I could see flashing lights everywhere. It looked like something out of a movie.

Suddenly, a few condors dove down, spiraling out of the air to attack a car! The birds actually attacked a vehicle, and they lifted it off the ground and into the air! It was unbelievable.

If I had been scared before, I was really terrified now. Here, inside Mt. Shasta, was a small city. How it got here, I hadn't a clue. I had never known that there was a city inside of a mountain.

But the city was under attack by giant condors, like the one that was carrying me at that very moment! Far below, people were running and screaming, trying to get away from the vicious, attacking birds. I snapped my head around and counted nearly a dozen of the giant, winged beasts. One of the condors landed on the giant 'H' of the Hollywood sign. The condor that was carrying the human still had the person in its clutches as it circled above the small city.

I saw a man emerge from a building, and he immediately began running down a street. Suddenly, one of the condors in the air folded its wings and dove straight at the man! It happened so fast that there was no way the man was going to be able to get out of the way. Besides . . . the man didn't even know that the condor was attacking!

"Watch out!" I screamed as loud as I could. *"He's coming after you! WATCH OUT!"*

But if he heard me, he didn't pay any attention. He just kept running down the street.

The attacking condor spread its massive wings and extended its legs out. I saw its claws open up.

The man on the ground wouldn't stand a chance.

But the attack never came.

At the very last possible second, a loud, booming voice echoed through the giant cavern.

"CUT! THAT'S A WRAP! EVERYBODY TAKE TWENTY FOR LUNCH!"

Sirens stopped blaring. Flashing lights blinked out. People came out of houses and cars. Stadium lights clicked on, and the entire cavern was bathed in bright white light.

What on earth is going on here? I wondered.

One by one, the condors that had been circling above the city began to swoop down. The one that had been carrying the person soared down to the ground, gently dropped the man onto the ground, then flew off, only to land on a long bar that was near a white trailer. Other condors had landed on the same perch, and more were arriving.

Suddenly, the condor that was carrying me began to descend. The bird circled around and around, expertly twisting and soaring lower and lower. In one single motion, it placed me on the ground and loosened its grip on my forearms. I let go, and the condor flew off, joining the other condors on the perch by the white trailer. Now that I was on the ground, I could see letters on the trailer. They read:

SCARYWORKS MOVIE COMPANY

There were several other white trailers nearby, and all of them had signs printed on them that said the same thing.

"What is this place?" I wondered aloud.

There were about a hundred people milling about. Some were in small groups, talking and laughing. Not far away, I saw a man carrying a clipboard and a megaphone. He had a beard and was wearing a baseball cap, and he looked like he might be in charge, so I started walking toward him.

All around me, people were busy. I saw a woman wearing a headset. She was carrying a camera on her shoulder. As I looked around, I could see more cameras. Some were seated on tripods, others were being carried by people.

I walked up to the man with the clipboard and the megaphone.

"What is going on here?" I asked.

The man turned and looked at me. "It's lunch break. Why?"

"No," I said, sweeping my arm in the air. "All of this. What's going on?"

"You know perfectly well," the man replied, staring at me. "We're making a movie. Now . . . you'd better hurry on and get your lunch. We've got a busy afternoon ahead."

"But I'm not a part of the movie," I said. "I was kidnapped by one of those things." I pointed to the row of motionless condors perched near the trailer.

The man looked at me strangely, and I explained how we'd been attacked in the forest, and how we learned to control the condor with Cameron's remote control. And I told him how Cameron had lost control of the condor, and how it had carried me through the tunnel into Mt. Shasta.

"That's very strange," the man said. "I know that we've been having some trouble with a couple of the mechanical birds, but I didn't think they were able to get out of the mountain. You see, they're programmed to be able to fly around on their own, but they shouldn't be picking up people unless they're guided by the condor operators."

"Condor operators?" I asked.

"Yes. You see—"

Suddenly, I gasped, causing the man to stop in mid-sentence. Twenty feet behind the man, I saw something . . . no—some*one*—that nearly made me faint.

21

Walking toward us was Arnold Shortenbigger, the famous movie star! I'm sure you've heard of him. And right behind him was another famous actor, Sylvester Malone! And the two famous sister/actresses, Mary Ash and Kately! I couldn't believe it! They were actually walking right up to us!

"Mr. Spellbird," Arnold said, "we have a few questions about the scene coming up."

Mr. Spellbird?!?! I thought. *Why . . . he must be Steven Spellbird, the famous movie director!*

The three men and the two girls spoke for a moment, and then Arnold Shortenbigger, Sylvester Malone, and Mary Ash and Kately walked off.

"Sorry about that," the man said to me. "Now . . . where were we?"

"You're Mr. Spellbird! You're the famous director!" I suddenly blurted out.

The man smiled. "Well, I don't know about that. But yes, my name is Steven Spellbird."

"I knew it! You're making a movie!"

"That's right," he said. "It's called *Revenge of the Condors.*"

"But how did you get all of this equipment here?" I asked. "There are homes and trailers and everything."

"There is a tunnel over there that leads into this giant cavern. Not many people know about this place. The tunnel is big enough to drive our semi trucks through. We spent months bringing in our equipment and materials and building the set."

"But why here?" I asked. "How come you didn't film the movie in Hollywood?"

"That's the tricky part," Mr. Spellbird explained. "You see, there is another movie company called *Terror Pictures, Incorporated,* that doesn't want us to make this movie. They know that it will be a blockbuster, and they won't be able to compete against it. By filming *Revenge of the Condors* in this giant cave, we can keep the production under wraps."

"Do you think this other movie company is going to try and stop you from making your movie?" I asked.

Mr. Spellbird nodded. "I am certain of it," he replied. "If they have a chance to stop us, they will."

All of a sudden, the door of a nearby trailer flew open. A man appeared.

"Mr. Spellbird!" he shouted. "You'd better come and see this!"

Mr. Spellbird broke into a jog, heading for the trailer. I didn't know what else to do, so I followed him.

And what I saw inside the trailer was *incredible*.

22

Inside the trailer were twelve computers, side by side, on a long table that was against the far wall. There was a person seated in front of each computer. In front of each person was a computer keyboard and what looked like a joystick game controller.

"What's wrong?" Mr. Spellbird asked.

A woman sitting at a computer turned. "Two of the condors have malfunctioned and have left the movie set," she said. "We lost control of them a while back. We regained control of one and brought it back."

"That was the one that brought me here!" I exclaimed.

"It's possible," the woman replied. "But the other one is still missing. We're trying to locate it with our tracking system, but we haven't had much luck yet."

"That's probably the other one we saw," I said to Mr. Spellbird. "My brother and I saw two condors."

"Who is she?" a man snapped. He had been standing back, watching everyone, and I hadn't noticed him until now. He didn't look really friendly.

"She's a friend," Mr. Spellbird said.

"We shouldn't have unauthorized people here in the condor command center," he said.

"We have bigger problems," Mr. Spellbird replied. "We've got to find that missing condor."

A man seated at a computer spoke up. "I was in charge of that particular bird," he said. "I was controlling it over the movie set, when it suddenly just flew off on its own. I didn't have any control over it."

"See if you can bring it up on the remote view," Mr. Spellbird ordered.

"Yes, sir," the man replied, and he began tapping at the keys and working with the joystick.

"Each one of the condors have video cameras implanted in their eyes," Mr. Spellbird explained to me. "The person at the computer controls the condor by seeing what the bird sees. It's displayed on the computer screen."

The man shook his head. Before him, the computer screen remained blank.

"I'm not getting anything," he said.

"Keep trying," Mr. Spellbird said. "We've got to find that condor."

The man continued working at the computer.

"It's no use," the man standing behind us said. "We're wasting a lot of time." Then he stormed off, flinging the door open and leaving in a huff.

"Who's he?" I asked.

"That's Mr. Flooster. He's in charge of all of the condors and the controllers. Don't mind him. He's just under a lot of pressure."

All of a sudden the computer screen blinked to life.

"I think we're getting something," the man said.

Then, a picture appeared on the screen. It was Mt. Shasta. I could make out the forest beneath the mountain, and the blue sky above.

"That's it!" the man said. "It's our missing condor!"

It was really kind of cool. I was looking through the eyes of a condor . . . which really weren't eyes at all . . . but a video camera.

"Can you bring him in?" Mr. Spellbird asked.

The man shook his head. "I'm trying," he said, as he moved the joystick around. "But it's not working.

We have a video feed, but I don't have any control over the bird."

"Keep trying," Mr. Spellbird said. "That thing is dangerous on its own."

We watched the screen, and Mt. Shasta loomed closer and closer with each passing second.

All of a sudden, the mountain disappeared, and we were looking at trees, and the base of the mountain.

And something else.

There was a small speck on the ground. It was moving. At first, I thought it might be a deer.

But as the condor swooped lower, faster and faster, I could make out the figure on the ground.

It wasn't a deer.

It was Cameron . . . *and the condor was attacking!*

23

"You've got to do something!" I suddenly shrieked. "That's Cameron! That's my brother!"

"I'm doing the best I can," the man at the computer said. "But the bird is malfunctioning. I'm trying to override its programming, but it isn't working!"

As I watched in horror, I could see Cameron walking toward the mountain. He had his back to the condor, and he had no idea that the bird was coming.

"Run, Cameron, run!" I shouted. Which was kind of silly, because I knew he couldn't hear me.

"Wait!" the man said. "I'm regaining control! Hold on!"

He worked furiously at his computer. With one hand, he tapped at the keyboard, and with the other, he twisted and turned the joystick.

But it was too late. The condor was already upon Cameron, and I could only watch as the bird reached out with its claws and snatched up Cameron by the leg!

"You've got to stop it!" I cried. "That's my brother!"

"One more second!" the man exclaimed.

On the computer screen, Cameron had vanished. The bird was in flight, rising above the trees.

"Where's . . . where's my brother?" I stammered. Tears welled up in my eyes. Sure, my brother can be a pest, but I would never, ever want him to get hurt.

"The bird still has hold of him," the man at the computer said. "But don't worry . . . I've got him now. I've got control of the condor."

"Can you bring him here?" I asked. "He has to know that I'm all right."

"I'll have to take him all the way to the other side of the mountain," the man said. "That's the only way to get into the cavern."

"No," I said, shaking my head. "There's a tunnel right up there." I pointed to the mountain that filled the computer screen. "You can't see it until you get really close. That's how the condor brought me here."

The man guided the condor around the ledge. Sure enough, the tunnel appeared.

"Man, my brother has got to be freaking out right about now," I said.

Suddenly, the screen went almost dark as the bird flew into the tunnel. I could see rock walls on either side.

"That's strange," I said.

"What's strange?" Mr. Spellbird replied.

"When the condor carried me through the tunnel, it was pitch black. I couldn't see a thing. But now, through the camera in the condor, I can see the walls of the tunnel."

"The cameras in each bird are very sensitive to light," the man controlling the condor answered. "It makes them easier to control in low light. It's almost like night-vision goggles that allow you to see in the dark."

Suddenly, the cavern appeared on the computer monitor. I spun and darted out of the trailer.

High above, the condor appeared . . . carrying Cameron upside down! He was shrieking at the top of his lungs.

"Put me down!" he was saying. *"Put me down, you fake-feathered flea-bitten bird! Put me DOWN!"*

The condor soared in circles, slowly descending. When he was low enough to hear, I shouted up to him.

"Cameron!" I yelled. "Don't worry! You're going to be okay!"

"Melanie!" he shouted back. "I thought you were a goner!"

The condor swooped low, lower still, and dropped Cameron to the ground. Because the bird had him by the leg, Cameron landed on his head. But he wasn't hurt.

He stood up and brushed himself off as I rushed up to him.

"Are you all right?" I asked.

"Yeah," he replied. "I am now." He stuffed his hands into his front pockets. "Hey!" he said angrily. "I lost my gold! It probably fell out when that bird picked me up!"

"A lot worse things could have happened," I said.

"Yeah, I guess so," Cameron replied. "Are you okay?"

"I'm fine," I answered, and I immediately explained what was going on, telling him about the two condors that were malfunctioning.

"So, all of this," he said, looking around, "all of this is one big movie set?"

"That's right," I said with a nod. "And guess what? Arnold Shortenbigger, Sylvester Malone, and Mary Ash and Kately are the stars!"

"No way!" Cameron gaped.

"I saw them a few minutes ago," I said. "They were five feet from me."

The door of the trailer suddenly opened, and Mr. Spellbird appeared. He raised the megaphone to his mouth. "Okay everyone," he boomed. "Take your places! This is going to be an important scene!"

We walked over to him, and I introduced Cameron.

"I'm sorry about this whole mess," he said. "And I'm glad you weren't hurt."

"That's okay," Cameron said. "Actually, now that we're here, it's kind of cool."

Mr. Spellbird's eyes suddenly lit up. "Hey," he said. "I've got a question for the two of you."

And when he told us about his idea, I couldn't believe my own ears!

24

"How would you kids like a small role in the movie?" he asked.

Cameron and I gasped.

"You . . . you mean . . . to be a part of the actual movie?" I stammered.

"Yeah," Mr. Spellbird replied. "We're shooting the final scene, where Mary Ash and Kately are trapped in a car that is being attacked by condors. Arnold Shortenbigger and Sylvester Malone save them just in time. Why don't we have you two in the car with Mary Ash and Kately?"

"You . . . you mean it?" Cameron stuttered.

"Sure," Mr. Spellbird said. "In fact, the original script called for two kids to be in the car with the twin sisters. But the kids were sick today. You guys can take their place, if you want. Think about it for a minute, and I'll be right back." He hurried off.

"Melanie!" Cameron said. "We're going to be movie stars!"

"Not so fast," I said. "What time is it?"

Cameron looked at his watch. "Two-thirty. We still have a lot of time before we have to be back to camp."

"But we have a long hike back," I said.

"We'll make it in time," Cameron said. "It can't take too long to film the last scene. It would be really super cool! We'll be movie stars!"

"All right," I said. "Let's do it!"

And so, we told Mr. Spellbird that we would love to help, and be a part of *Revenge of the Condors*.

"Great," he said. "Now . . . there are a couple of people you'll need to meet. Follow me."

We did as we were asked. All around us, the set was coming to life. People with cameras and lights were scurrying everywhere. Other people were shouting orders. Everyone was getting into position.

We walked over to a long trailer. There were four people standing in front of it.

"We have a couple of stand-ins," Mr. Spellbird announced to the four. "This is Melanie and Cameron Doyle. Melanie and Cameron . . . meet Arnold

Shortenbigger, Sylvester Malone, and Mary Ash and Kately."

I was so overwhelmed that I couldn't move. I couldn't even speak.

"How do you do?" Mr. Shortenbigger said. Mr. Malone and the two sisters smiled and nodded.

Mr. Spellbird went over the scene with us, and explained what we would be doing. Actually, it sounded kind of simple. We would be in the car with Mary Ash and Kately, and the car would suddenly be attacked by condors. Arnold Shortenbigger and Sylvester Malone would arrive just in time to drive the condors off and save us.

Simple.

But sometimes, making movies can be dangerous.

Sometimes, things don't go as planned.

And today, while filming the last scene of the movie, something was going to go horribly wrong.

I was so excited I could hardly stand it! We were going to be in a movie! And not just any movie, either. A big-time movie, with big-time movie stars!

The scene that we were going to be in was right at the end of the movie. Mary Ash would drive the car, and Kately would ride in the passenger seat. Cameron and I rode in the back seat.

When we got into the car, I was really nervous. After all, I've never been around movie stars before.

But Mary Ash and Kately were really cool. They told us what to do and how to act. They explained that the car would stall, and then the condors would attack. Then Arnold Shortenbigger and Sylvester Malone would arrive on motorcycles and fight off the condors. Then, we would all leap out of the car and run to a nearby building while Arnold and Sylvester battled the condors.

"Okay, everyone!" Mr. Spellbird's voice boomed through the megaphone. Cameron and I were already in the back seat.

"You guys ready?" Kately asked us.

"Yeah," I replied.

"I am!" Cameron said. "This is going to be cool!" Mr. Spellbird's voice boomed again. "Ready . . . set . . . *action!*"

The car began to move down the street. As I looked around, I could see people busily operating cameras and lights. A few condors flew, soaring above the car we were riding in.

"Mr. Spellbird is signaling us to pull the car over," Mary Ash said. "This is where the car stalls out."

She steered the car to the side of the road.

"Look panicky," Kately said, and we all began acting like we were in a lot of trouble. Soon, a condor flew over the hood of the car, and then another. Suddenly, there were several of them swarming around the car, circling like hornets.

"This is awesome!" Cameron exclaimed.

"Better than awesome," I said.

"Here comes Arnold and Sylvester!" Mary Ash said, glancing into the rearview mirror. I turned around and saw the two men on motorcycles. They were a couple blocks away, and condors were swooping down at them. It was hard to believe that, not far away, there were twelve people sitting at computers, controlling the movements of the giant birds.

A condor grabbed the front bumper of the car and began to fly up. The bird wasn't strong enough to lift the car up by itself, but it sure tried hard. If I didn't know that this was a movie, I would have been terrified!

Arnold Shortenbigger and Sylvester Malone rode up on their motorcycles, just like they were supposed to. By now, there were five or six condors attacking our car. It was going to be fun to watch the two movie stars battle the giant creatures.

Suddenly, from behind the big Hollywood sign, there was a huge explosion! Everything seemed to shake . . . the ground, the car . . . even the buildings around us. Arnold and Sylvester spun to see what had happened, but it was already too late. All of the lights flickered and went out . . . and the entire cavern plunged into total darkness!

26

"What . . . what happened?" I stammered.

"I don't know," one of the girls in the front seat replied. In the darkness, I couldn't see, so I didn't know if it was Mary Ash or Kately that answered me.

I could hear people yelling, and I heard Mr. Spellbird shout something about a flashlight. Soon, tiny beams began appearing. I could see shadows and silhouettes of people scurrying about. Arnold Shortenbigger came up to the car and knocked on the window.

"Are you all right in there?" he asked.

We all nodded, and Arnold walked off.

"What do we do?" Cameron asked.

"Let's just stay here," Mary Ash said, and she turned on the car lights. That was pretty smart, because the headlights were very bright. Soon, a few more car lights blinked on.

After a few minutes, Mr. Spellbird came up to the car carrying a flashlight. He leaned over, and Kately rolled down the window.

"Had a searchlight blow up," he explained. "I guess it got too hot. No big problem to worry about. If you guys just want to sit tight for a few minutes, we'll have it repaired. Then we'll shoot the scene over again."

That sounded fine with us, and, true to Mr. Spellbird's word, the lights began working only a few minutes later. Mr. Spellbird told everyone to get into position, and soon, we picked up right where we left off . . . when Arnold Shortenbigger and Sylvester Malone had just arrived on their motorcycles.

The scene went perfect. The two men fought off the condors. Suddenly, Arnold flung open the car door and ordered us to run to a nearby house.

We piled out of the car. Just above our heads, condors flapped their wings and hovered around the car. We ducked down and ran as fast as we could, and we didn't stop until we were inside the house.

Mary Ash, Kately, Cameron and I watched through a window. It was fascinating to see how a movie scene was filmed. What was really surprising is the amount of people that were working behind the scenes. It sure took a lot of people to make a movie!

Soon, Arnold Shortenbigger and Sylvester Malone had fought off the remaining condors. A searchlight was trained on them as they stood in the street. Mr. Spellbird's voice came through the megaphone.

"Okay, hold it . . . one more second . . . cut! Great job, everybody! That's a wrap!"

People started to cheer and applaud. The filming was over. We walked out the front door of the house as the condors began flying to their perch near the trailer. I saw people shaking hands and slapping each other on the back.

We said good-bye to Mary Ash and Kately. I wanted to say good-bye to Arnold Shortenbigger and Sylvester Malone, but I didn't see them around anywhere.

Mr. Spellbird was standing over by a trailer, talking with several people. We waited until he was done to speak to him.

Finally, he saw us and he came over to us.

"Hey," he said, shaking my hand. "You guys did great!" He shook Cameron's hand.

"Thank you," I said.

Mr. Spellbird shook his head and smiled. "When that searchlight blew up, I thought we were in a lot of trouble. I'm glad things worked out the way they did."

But our adventure wasn't over yet. Mr. Spellbird didn't know it, and neither did we . . . but trouble was on the way.

Trouble . . . with a capital 'T'.

27

The cavern was abuzz with activity. Everywhere, people were busy dismantling sets and taking apart things. Even the houses were being taken apart, wall by wall, and loaded onto semi-trucks.

"What's next?" I asked Mr. Spellbird. "Is the movie going to be out next week?"

Mr. Spellbird laughed. "I'm afraid there's still a lot of work to do," he said. "You see, now that we have all of the footage filmed, we have to take it to our studios in Hollywood and edit all of the scenes together. It's going to take weeks and weeks. The movie won't be released to theaters until six months from now, so we're ahead of schedule."

"I can't wait to see it!" Cameron said.

"Yes, I think it's going to be a great movie," Mr. Spellbird agreed. "And I'm sure glad that we were able to film it without interference from anyone at Terror Pictures, Incorporated. They sure didn't want us making this movie. But now, it's too late. They can't stop us now."

"Where does all of this stuff go?" I asked, looking around at all of the things that were being taken down.

"All of it will go back into storage," Mr. Spellbird answered. "We have huge storage buildings in Hollywood, Los Angeles . . . all over. Some of the things we'll use again for other movies. Like the big 'Hollywood' letters on the other side of the cavern. We'll be using those in a movie next year."

"I don't suppose you'd give me one of those condors," Cameron said.

"Cameron!" I scolded.

My brother shrugged. "Doesn't hurt to ask."

Again, Mr. Spellbird laughed. "While I'm sure you would have a lot of fun with one of those birds, I'm afraid I can't give one to you. Each condor costs over one million dollars."

One million dollars! Holy cow! That would mean that it cost over twelve million dollars . . . just for the condors!

"Making a movie is a costly venture," Mr. Spellbird added. "It takes a great deal of money to make a movie such as *Revenge of the Condors.*"

"Yeah, I guess so," Cameron said, but I could tell he was a little disappointed. I knew he was looking forward to taking one of the mechanical condors to school and showing it to his friends.

"Well, I've got to get back to work," Mr. Spellbird finished. "I've got—"

And that's when disaster struck.

There was a loud crash from a nearby garage. Suddenly, a red truck came crashing through the garage door! The door wasn't even open, but the truck caused the garage door to splinter and fall apart.

Worse yet, the truck was wildly out of control . . . and it was headed right for us!

28

"Out of the way!" Mr. Spellbird screamed. *"Hurry!"*

He pushed us to the side, just as the big truck flew past. Then there was a squealing of brakes, and the truck skidded to a stop. The driver's side window rolled down, and Mr. Flooster—the man who was in charge of the condor controllers—appeared.

"What are you doing, driving a vehicle like that?!?!" Mr. Spellbird demanded. "You could have killed somebody!"

"It's my own business how I drive," Mr. Flooster snapped. "The important thing is that this movie will never make it to theaters!"

"What are you talking about?!?!" Mr. Spellbird asked.

"This movie!" he pointed to the back of the truck. "I've got all of the film footage in the back of this truck, and it won't even make it to the editing room!"

"You . . . you traitor!" Mr. Spellbird shrieked. "I paid you good money to put together and manage a team of people who could control those condors!"

"Yeah, well, *Terror Pictures* paid me *more* money to stop you from making this movie. I tried to reprogram the condors so they wouldn't operate right, but that plan didn't work. When I knew that the filming was about wrapped up, I rigged one of the searchlights to explode. That created a lot of confusion, and it gave me time to load all of the film canisters into the truck."

"You're a fiend!" Mr. Spellbird shouted angrily.

"I'm a rich fiend," Mr. Flooster snapped. "Now, I'm going to leave here, and if anyone follows me, I'm going to drive this truck into the lake. It'll ruin all of the film for good!" And with that, he stepped on the gas. The truck tore off, heading for the tunnel that would lead out of Mt. Shasta and down the side of the mountain.

Mr. Spellbird pulled out his cellular phone and called the police. He told them what had happened, but the police said that there was no way they would be able to get a police car out in time to stop Mr. Flooster.

126

Mr. Spellbird called an emergency meeting with all of his assistants, and everybody tried coming up with ideas to stop Mr. Flooster.

Someone suggested chasing after him.

"No," Mr. Spellbird said. "It's too dangerous. Besides . . . we all heard what he said. He'll destroy all of the film if he knows he's being followed. We've spent millions of dollars over the past few months. If that film gets destroyed, the movie is done for."

Nobody had any practical suggestions as to what could or should be done. For the most part, Cameron and I just listened to everyone discuss the matter. I felt really bad for Mr. Spellbird, because I know that he'd worked so hard on *Revenge of the Condors*.

And that's when I had an idea.

A *good* idea. At least I thought it was good.

I raised my hand. "Um . . . I . . . I . . . um, have an idea, if anyone would like to hear it."

No one said a word, so I continued, and explained what I was thinking.

Jaws dropped. Eyes popped. Mr. Spellbird clenched his fists. "Yes!" he cried. "Melanie! That's a brilliant idea!"

My idea was quite simple. So simple, in fact, that I
was surprised that no one else had come up with it.

Here's what would happen:

The twelve condors would take flight, each of
them controlled by the people manning the computers.
They would fly out of Mt. Shasta through the tunnel
that we'd flown in through. Since the controllers could
see what the condor was seeing through the video
cameras, maybe they could locate the truck that Mr.
Flooster had taken. Mr. Flooster wouldn't be looking
in the sky . . . he'd be looking in his mirror to see if
anyone was following him. All twelve of the condors
could swoop down at the same time, lift the truck up
into the air, and carry it back to Mt. Shasta.

Things were put into motion. People scrambled, and the condor controllers took their positions. Mr. Spellbird went around and spoke to everyone, making sure each person knew exactly what they were supposed to do.

"Okay everyone," he said, addressing everyone in the trailer, "we need to keep the birds together in a tight formation. Keep them high in the sky, until we're ready to dive down to the truck. Does anyone have any questions?"

A man at a computer spoke up. "That truck and all of that film is going to be really heavy," he said. "We've never lifted anything that big before. Are you sure the twelve birds can pick it up?"

"I'm pretty sure they can," Mr. Spellbird replied. "Besides . . . it's a risk I'm willing to take. We've got to stop Flooster, and we've got to get that film back safely. Any other questions?"

Nobody spoke.

"Okay," Mr. Spellbird said. "Let's get those birds up in the air."

The men and women at the computers began tapping away at their keyboards . . . but they all started looking confused. Through the trailer window, I could see the condors still on their perch. None of them had moved.

"Something's wrong," one of the men said.

"What is it?" Mr. Spellbird asked.

"The condors," the man replied. "They aren't responding."

"Is something wrong with the computers?" Mr. Spellbird asked.

"No," a woman answered. "The computers are fine. For whatever reason, the condors aren't responding to our radio signals."

Mr. Spellbird walked over to the table and inspected a rack of equipment. Then he threw his hands in the air.

"That rat fink figured us out!" he said angrily. "Look! He's taken the transmitter that sends the radio signal to the condors!"

Sure enough, there was an empty space in the rack where the transmitter should have been.

"How could he have taken it right from under your noses?" Mr. Spellbird asked.

"We all took a coffee break when the filming was complete," a man answered. "No one was in the trailer at that time. He must have taken it then."

"We'll never stop him now, I'm afraid," Mr. Spellbird said in frustration. "I guess we'd better face the facts. Flooster has gotten away, and *Revenge of the Condors* will never make it to the big screen."

"I have an idea," Cameron said quietly, and suddenly, I knew what he meant.

"If you have an idea," Mr. Spellbird said, "I'd really like to know what it is."

And so, Cameron reached into his back pocket . . . and pulled out his remote control.

30

"What is that?" Mr. Spellbird asked.

"It's my remote control for my airplane. I used it to control the condor, after I had found the right frequency. All we would have to do is—"

"—change the radio frequency in each of the condors!" Mr. Spellbird said. He looked over at a man seated at a computer. "Terry!" he said. "You know how the transmitter operates. Could we wire this remote control into the computer banks? Would it work?"

"Yeah, probably, if the Condors were on the same radio frequency," he said.

"Let's move!" Mr. Spellbird said. "We don't have a minute to waste!"

Several people ran out of the trailer to attend to the condors. Each bird would have to have its radio frequency changed, just like Cameron had done with the bird in the forest. Cameron handed his remote control to one of the men in the trailer, and he got to work wiring it into the equipment rack.

While the man was wiring Cameron's remote, Cameron started talking to him.

"One thing I don't understand," Cameron said. "When we changed the frequency in the condor, I got it to work with my remote control. Then, when it was up above the trees, my remote didn't work. How come?"

The man shook his head. "I don't know what Mr. Flooster did to those two condors, but he probably tried to re-program their own computer chips. However, the signal that we transmit over is very strong. I think our signal overrode your signal. Although we didn't necessarily have control of the bird, each of the condors is preprogrammed to return to Mt. Shasta and hover in the air . . . just in case we lose our signal. Which, of course, is what happened with those two condors. Mr. Flooster tried to mess up the birds, but his plan didn't work as well as he'd hoped."

That made sense. I was wondering why the condor that was carrying me had brought me into Mt. Shasta when no one had any control over it.

"Condors are ready, Mr. Spellbird!" someone shouted from outside the trailer.

"Transmitter is wired, Mr. Spellbird!" the man working on the equipment rack said.

"Power up, and let's get these birds in the air!" Mr. Spellbird replied.

Everyone went back to their positions. The men and women that operated the condors took their seats at their computers and began tapping away at their keyboards.

Again, nothing happened.

"Now what's wrong?" Mr. Spellbird asked.

"The birds still aren't receiving a signal, sir," someone said.

"But the transmitter is wired in! The frequencies in each condor has been changed! What could possibly be wrong?!?!"

I leaned over to Cameron and whispered into his ear.

"Melanie!" he exclaimed. "I'll bet you're right!"

"I think I am," I replied.

"Hey, if one of you two know how you can fix this, we'd like to know," Mr. Spellbird said. "Time is wasting, and Mr. Flooster is getting away!"

Cameron walked over to the small remote control. Now, it had wires coming out of it that were connected to the computer mainframe.

He smiled.

"Watch this," he said with a smirk.

31

While everyone was watching, Cameron reached down, glanced up, and said smartly, *"you forgot to turn it on."*

He flipped the power switch.

The effect was immediate. Outside the trailer, condors came to life, flapping their wings and flying off their perches.

"That's more like it!" Mr. Spellbird shouted. "Let's hustle, people! Let's get those birds out there!"

Within a few seconds, all of the condors were in the air. All of the men and women controlling the birds were hard at work, watching their screens, tapping into their keyboards and working with their joysticks. It was really cool to watch.

Mr. Spellbird walked out of the trailer, and Cameron and I followed. We watched the condors circle, rising higher and higher, higher still. One by one, each bird left the cavern by going through the same tunnel Cameron and I had been brought through.

"They're off," Mr. Spellbird said, and he walked back into the trailer. Again, we followed.

The condor controllers were focused at their computers. On each screen, we could see what each bird was 'seeing' through the video camera. At the moment, most of the computer screens showed only the dark walls of the tunnel. Occasionally, another condor would come into view, which would only make sense. If a condor was flying in front of the bird that was being watched on the monitor, it would only be logical that it would show up on the computer screen.

It didn't take the condors long to emerge from the tunnel. Soon, all of the computer screens displayed blue sky and lush, green forests.

"Perfect," Mr. Spellbird said. "Now . . . bring the birds around to the other side of the mountain, to where the entrance of the ground tunnel is. As soon as the mountain road comes into sight, follow it. We've got to stop Mr. Flooster!"

It took a couple of minutes for the condors to reach the other side of the mountain, but soon, a well-worn dirt road came into view.

"There!" someone seated at a computer exclaimed. "There it is!"

"Higher," Mr. Spellbird said. "His truck will be easier to see if the condors are higher up."

No one said a word. They simply followed Mr. Spellbird's orders, typing commands into the keyboards, maneuvering the birds with their joysticks.

And it wasn't long before Mr. Flooster's truck was spotted. Several of the operators saw it at the same time.

"There it is!"

My eyes darted from screen to screen. For the most part, each screen had pretty much the same thing to see, but some showed the scene from a slightly different angle. I caught a flash of red on the computer directly in front of me. It was the truck Mr. Flooster had taken, all right . . . and he was really moving fast.

"Okay, okay," Mr. Spellbird said. "Keep the birds in a tight formation and bring them down. You're going to pick up the truck just like you did in a scene in the movie."

As I watched the screens, the trees rapidly drew closer, and so did the red truck.

"Everybody ready?"

Murmurs of agreement came from the condor controllers.

"All right, then," Mr. Spellbird said. "Go get that truck!"

Were twelve condors really going to be able to lift up a truck off the ground and carry it back to Mt. Shasta?

I had my doubts.

Regardless, we were about to find out.

32

The condors attacked, swooping down on the red truck, swarming the vehicle, getting into position. The truck suddenly swerved to the other side of the road, then back again.

"He's trying to shake them off!" Mr. Spellbird said. "Stay with him! Don't let him get away! And don't let him do anything that will damage the film in the back of the truck!"

The scene in the trailer was chaotic. The condor controllers were each focused at their own computer, furiously working to keep each condor on target.

And it was difficult to see what was going on. Since there was so much rapid movement as the condors each tried to grasp a part of the truck, it was hard to know exactly what was happening. Many of the computer screens displayed jerky, bouncing images.

But on one screen, we caught a glimpse of Mr. Flooster's face . . . and boy, did he look mad!

"You've got to stop him!" Mr. Spellbird cried. "Get those birds into position!"

"Almost there, sir," a woman called out.

"Do you really think this is going to work?" Cameron asked.

I nodded. "If you would have asked me that yesterday, I would have said no," I replied. "But after what I've seen today, I really think that they can pull this off. Those mechanical condors are super-strong."

We continued watching the monitors, trying to make sense of the confusing, flashing images.

"Ready!" a man suddenly shouted.

"Take 'er up!" Mr. Spellbird ordered.

Not one second later, the scenes on the computer screens began to change. Oh, the images were still very bouncy and hard to make out, but I could clearly see that the truck had been picked up a few feet off the ground.

"It's going to work!" I exclaimed.

And we all thought it would . . . until Mr. Flooster did something that no one had planned for.

33

The truck had been lifted only a few feet off the ground, when all of a sudden the driver's side door opened . . . and Mr. Flooster jumped out! He landed on the dirt road and began running. If he would have waited a few seconds more, the truck would have been too high for him to jump.

"He's getting away!" Cameron cried.

"Not for long," a man at his computer said with confidence. "I'll get him!"

We watched as he expertly guided his condor from the truck, which was now rapidly being lifted high into the sky. I saw Mr. Flooster come into view on the computer screen. He was running down the road, turning his head every few seconds to look up. When he saw the condor coming his way, he began running faster.

"Get him!" I snarled.

The condor dove, and Mr. Flooster tried to dart out of the way. The condor, however, was quicker, and the bird spun around, and, using its strong legs and claws, seized Mr. Flooster by the shoulders.

"You did it!" Cameron cried.

"Okay everybody," Mr. Spellbird said, "bring them home. I'm going to go to the tunnel entrance and greet the truck and the traitor."

Mr. Spellbird left the trailer, followed by Cameron and me. Several other people that weren't working on the computers also followed.

A dirt road wound around several trailers in the cavern. We followed it until we saw a large opening, spilling bright daylight into the cavern. Warm, fresh air breezed against my cheeks.

And suddenly, we were outside of the mountain. Birds sang from trees, and the sky was a perfect blue without a single cloud.

We scanned the sky for the truck and Mr. Flooster. After a few minutes, a large speck came into view in the distance, along with a tinier speck.

"There they are!" Mr. Spellbird said, pointing into the sky.

As we watched, the objects drew nearer. I wished that I had a camera! It was really strange to see a bunch of birds carrying a truck so high in the sky. It looked like something out of . . . well . . . something out of a movie.

It didn't take long for the truck and Mr. Flooster to be carried to the mountain. In a few minutes, the truck was right above us. The condor carrying Mr. Flooster was higher up in the sky.

"Everybody back," Mr. Spellbird ordered. "Let's give them some room."

We all backed up into a semicircle as the truck began to lower. I could hear the heavy beating of wings as the condors flapped and guided the truck to the ground.

And suddenly, there it was, safe on the ground. As the truck was set down, the condors flew up and off, soaring up into the sky above.

Mr. Flooster was next. He was being carried by a single condor, and he wasn't liking it one bit. He was yelling and kicking and making a fuss.

A siren sounded from far off, but it was getting louder, drawing nearer. The condor carrying Mr. Flooster set him down just as two police cars arrived, lights flashing, sirens whooping. The sirens stopped, but the lights continued to flash as two police officers got out of each vehicle.

"You should have filmed this part and put it in the movie," I said to Mr. Spellbird. He didn't say anything, but he laughed really hard.

The police took Mr. Flooster away. I imagined that he probably was in a *lot* of trouble.

But most important of all, Mr. Spellbird had the film back, and he couldn't have been happier. He made a quick inspection of the truck, just to make sure. After he was certain that all of the film canisters weren't damaged, he ordered one of his assistant directors to drive the truck back into the cavern.

Then he turned to us.

"And you guys," he said. "We wouldn't have been able to stop him if it wasn't for your help. But there's one more thing I'd like you to do."

And when he told us what it was, I couldn't speak. Neither could Cameron.

All we could do was stare, wide eyed, with our mouths open.

"Did you guys hear me?" Mr. Spellbird asked. "I said that I'd like you and your family to join me for the world premiere of *Revenge of the Condors* when it opens at the theater."

Again, I couldn't believe what I heard. *The world premiere!* I thought. *That would be awesome!*

I tried to answer by speaking, but my mouth wouldn't work. So I just slowly nodded my head.

"Excellent!" Mr. Spellbird said. "Just make sure you give your address to one of my assistants before you leave."

Suddenly, Cameron gasped. A look of horror swept over his face.

"Oh no!" he cried. "Oh no!"

34

"What is it?!?!" I asked. I was alarmed, too. Just seeing how terrified Cameron was made me frightened.

Cameron suddenly raised his arm and looked at his watch.

"It's four o'clock!" he exclaimed. "We're supposed to be back at camp right now!"

I gulped. Mom and Dad would be really worried, and we had no way of contacting them to let them know we were okay.

"Can someone drive us back to our camp?" I asked Mr. Spellbird.

"Yes, but the way these mountain roads twist and turn, it will take you over an hour," Mr. Spellbird replied.

Over an hour?!?! Mom and Dad would have called the police by then!

"We've got to get back to camp in a hurry," Cameron said.

Suddenly, a soaring condor caught my eye . . . and that gave me an idea.

"Mr. Spellbird! Do you think that we could borrow a couple of condors?"

Mr. Spellbird looked puzzled. "What for?"

Instantly, Cameron knew what I was talking about. "Two condors can fly us back to camp!" he exclaimed.

"Exactly!" I said. "That would be a lot faster than driving or hiking!"

"I guess that would be fine," Mr. Spellbird said.

"We need to talk to the condor operators," I said. "Since they'll be able to see through the video cameras in the condors, we'll have to tell them what to look for so they'll know our campsite when they see it."

We walked back into the cavern and made our way to the trailer. The condor controllers were still at their posts, guiding the condors into the cavern. Some of the birds had already landed at their perch beside the trailer.

Mr. Spellbird spoke with two of the controllers, explaining what we needed. I couldn't hear the conversation, but I saw the two men nodding their heads. Then they looked at Cameron and me, and waved us over.

"What does your camp look like?" one of the men asked.

"It has two blue tents," I replied. "And a white car. There's a stream real close to it, too."

"That shouldn't be too hard to find," he said. "Are you guys ready?"

"The sooner, the better," Cameron said, glancing at his watch again.

"Go stand outside the trailer," the man ordered, "and stand a few feet apart from each other. Raise your arms straight up into the air."

"Wait!" Mr. Spellbird said. "Your address! I need your address!"

I wrote it down on a piece of paper, and Mr. Spellbird put it in his pocket.

"Thank you again," he said.

"Hey, it was a lot of fun," I replied.

"See you at the world premiere," he said.

Then we walked out of the trailer and did what the man asked. We stood several feet away from each other and raised our hands into the air.

Inside the trailer, the two men took their seats at their computers. Two condors leapt from their perches and soared up into the air above us. As we watched, they hovered overhead, flapping their wings to remain steady. Gradually, they lowered, and soon, their claws were wrapped around my arms. Likewise, I gripped around the bird's legs and held on. I looked through the trailer window and nodded to the men at their computers.

And, for the second time that day, I was suddenly being lifted into the air by a giant condor!

Only this time, I wasn't as frightened. I just wanted to get back to camp as quickly as possible.

Just wait until Mom and Dad see us fly back to camp with two condors! Boy, were they in for a surprise!

We rose up, higher and higher. Beneath us in the cavern, we could see people working to take apart the movie sets. Far off, on the other side, the big HOLLYWOOD letters were being dismantled and loaded onto semi trucks.

Soon, we were near the top of the cavern, and the condor was carrying me into the tunnel that led out the side of Mt. Shasta. It was really dark, but only for less than a minute.

Then I was in sunshine again as the condor emerged from the tunnel. Cameron was right behind me.

"This is so coooooool!" I heard him shout, his voice muffled by the wind rushing past my ears.

We rose up high, and I scoured the ground far below, looking for our campsite . . . and it didn't take long to find it. The man controlling the condor must have spotted it, too, because I could feel myself suddenly swooping down. It was a really cool feeling. The bird soared with its wings extended, not flapping or anything. It was like having my own personal airplane.

Beneath us, I could see our two tents, along with our white car. We were coming in for a landing, and fast!

But there was no sign of Mom or Dad. Maybe they were in the tents.

And suddenly, I was on the ground. In one single motion the bird set me down, released my arms, and swooped away. Cameron was next, and the condor that had been carrying him flew off. We watched the two birds as they flew up into the air, finally disappearing over the trees.

I looked around. There was no sign of our parents.

"Mom?" I called out. "Dad?"

I peered into the tents.

No one.

"Man, I hope they didn't go looking for us," Cameron said.

I saw a movement in the woods by the stream.

"There they are!" Cameron exclaimed, and while we watched, Mom and Dad came through the trees. Mom was carrying our two canteens, and Dad was carrying my pan and my metal detector.

And they did *not* look happy.

35

"Man, I think we're really in for it this time," Cameron whispered. *"It's almost four-thirty. We're a half an hour late."*

"Where have you been?" Dad asked as they drew nearer.

I was about to answer, but I suddenly realized how silly I was going to sound. If I told them that we had been taken to Mt. Shasta by mechanical condors, and then we had a small part in an upcoming movie, they'd think I was crazy!

But it was the absolute truth . . . so that's what we told them. We explained everything to them—the condors, the mountain and the secret cavern inside, meeting Mr. Spellbird, along with Arnold

Shortenbigger, Sylvester Malone, and Mary Ash and Kately. We explained how Mr. Flooster had stolen the film, but the condors picked up his truck, along with Mr. Flooster, and brought them back to Mt. Shasta. Then the condors flew us back to our campsite.

Mom and Dad looked at us. They didn't smile at all. I couldn't tell if they were angry or not.

Mom put her hands on her hips. "And you expect us to believe *that?!?!*" she asked.

"It's the truth!" I protested.

"Condors? Movie stars? Really, Melanie . . . you don't have to make up stories."

"But I'm not making it up!"

"Your father and I were very worried. When we found your canteens and your pan and your metal detector, we thought you'd gotten lost. Next time, don't wander off so far. And if you're late again, don't make up wild stories."

"Wild stories?!?!" Cameron said.

Dad laughed. "You know, I was a bit worried when you hadn't returned by four o'clock. When we came back and saw you both standing here, I was relieved . . . and a little angry. But your story is so funny!"

"Funny?!?!" I said. "It's the truth!"

"Yeah, whatever," Dad snickered. "Now . . . go get cleaned up and ready for dinner."

No matter what we said, I knew that Mom and Dad would never believe us.

But six months later, that all changed.

And it started with a knock on our door.

36

We were all home. School had started back up, and I was in my bedroom working on homework. Cameron was watching television with Mom and Dad.

There was a knock on the door.

I heard Dad get up to answer it, and then I heard a man asking for Cameron and me. I got up and went into the living room.

There was a man in a black suit standing at the door. I had never seen him before, and I had no idea who he was.

"Melanie Doyle?" he asked.

I nodded. "Yeah?" I replied.

"I'm here to pick up you and your family."

"Pick us up?" Dad asked.

"Yes," the man responded. "Mr. Spellbird wishes you all to be his special guests at the world premiere of his new movie *Revenge of the Condors.*"

Mom and Dad looked at me, then at Cameron.

"See!" I blurted out. "We told you! We told you the truth!"

"What are you talking about?" Dad asked.

"When we went camping last summer!" Cameron said. "Remember when we were late getting back to camp, and we told you about the condors? You didn't believe us! But it's true! All of it!"

"Where is Mr. Spellbird?" I asked the man in the black suit.

He stepped away from the door, and parked by the curb was the biggest, longest black stretch limousine I had ever seen.

"Mr. Spellbird is waiting in the car," he replied.

It took a few minutes, but we finally convinced Mom and Dad that we had to go. The man in the black suit walked us to the limousine.

And I'll tell you one thing for sure: that car sure got a lot of attention! All of our neighbors were outside of their houses, staring at the car, wondering who was inside. When they saw us walk toward it, they all gasped. They couldn't believe that we were going to get inside!

"Right this way," the man in the black suit instructed, and he led us to a door at the back of the car.

I couldn't wait to see Mr. Spellbird again. Finally! Now Mom and Dad would *have* to believe us!

But when the man in the black suit opened the door, I was in for a shock . . . .

37

Mr. Spellbird was in the limousine, just as we expected.

But so was Arnold Shortenbigger, Sylvester Malone, and Mary Ash and Kately!

Dad and Mom recognized the movie stars instantly.

"Please," Mr. Spellbird said. "Come in. Ah, these people must be your parents."

We piled into the limousine and Mr. Spellbird introduced everyone to one another.

Mom and Dad were dumbfounded. They hadn't believed our story when we'd told them, and I guess that I couldn't blame them. But now we had the proof!

"Are we going to see the movie?" Cameron asked.

Mr. Spellbird nodded. "That's right," he replied.

"But . . . but I thought that you were going to mail us tickets or something," I said. "That's why you needed our address."

"I needed your address so I would know where to pick you up," he answered.

We talked and laughed while the limousine made its way through the city. It was really cool talking with the stars of the movie. They were real nice.

When we arrived at the theater, there were people everywhere. Cameras started flashing, people were waving. Security guards had to keep people back while the limousine pulled up to the theater. Television news cameras lined the sidewalk.

The man in the black suit that had been driving the limo got out, walked to the back of the car, and opened the door. Cameron stepped out first, then me, then Mom and Dad.

There were dozens of people all over the place! Flashbulbs were going off, people were cheering and applauding . . . it was crazy!

Then Mr. Spellbird emerged, followed by Arnold Shortenbigger, Sylvester Malone, and Mary Ash and Kately.

The crowd went wild. The stars signed some autographs as we made our way to the theater. Some people even asked *me* for my autograph!

Finally, we entered the movie theater. It was already filled with people. Mostly, special guests of Mr. Spellbird.

"This way," Mr. Spellbird said. "We have special balcony seats."

We followed him up a staircase and through a door, then down the balcony to our seats.

"I told you we were telling the truth!" I heard Cameron whisper to Mom and Dad. *"I told you!"*

We took our seats, and the movie began. It was incredible . . . and really scary. Mom and Dad couldn't believe it when they saw me and Cameron, along with Mary Ash and Kately in the car being attacked by condors. It was a great scene.

But the best part of all was a scene where a condor swooped out of a blue sky and attacked a boy on the side of a mountain!

"Hey!" Cameron hissed. *"That's me!"*

"It was a great shot," Mr. Spellbird said. "We decided to put it into the movie."

At the end of the show, everyone stood up and cheered. It was a great movie, filled with a lot of action and suspense.

And I was a part of it!

I heard a few people talking about their favorite parts, and how terrified they were when the condors had attacked. The movie looked very real.

Of course, we knew the secret. We knew that the condors weren't real . . . they were mechanical. But they sure looked real on the movie screen!

At school we became famous. When we had first told our friends about what had happened on our camping trip, none of them believed us. They all said that we were making it up.

But now everybody believed us! Everybody asked us questions. They wanted to know what it was like meeting famous movie stars, and what it was like to actually be in one of Steven Spellbird's films.

And everyone agreed that *Revenge of the Condors* was the scariest movie they'd ever seen.

Except for a new student in my class.

His name was Jim Newkirk, and he had just moved to Los Angeles from Nebraska. He was really kind of quiet and shy, but he was really interested in what had happened to us while camping in the foothills of Mt. Shasta. One day in the cafeteria, he came over and sat down across from me. He asked a lot of questions, and I talked with him for a while.

"Have you seen *Revenge of the Condors?*" I asked.

He nodded. "Yeah," he replied.

"Pretty scary, huh?" I said.

He agreed, but he had a strange look on his face.

"It was scary," he said. "But some things in real life are actually *scarier* than the movies."

"Like what?" I asked.

"Nightcrawlers," he replied.

I laughed so hard I almost choked on my sandwich.

"Nightcrawlers?!?!" I said. "You mean, like, *worms?"*

"Exactly," he said. "Big ones."

"You're afraid of . . . of *worms?"* I tried to keep from laughing, but it was hard.

He nodded. "Big nightcrawlers. You'd be afraid of them, too, if you saw them."

"I've never been afraid of a worm in my life," I said, "and I'm not going to start. Who in the world would be afraid of nightcrawlers?"

"Me," Jim replied. "And if you knew what I knew, you *would* be afraid."

"So tell me," I said.

Jim shook his head. "You wouldn't believe me. Nobody does."

"Hey, I know how that feels," I replied. "Nobody believed our condor story . . . at first. Now they do. Go ahead. Tell me."

"It'll take a while," he replied. "Meet me on the playground after school and I'll tell you then."

"Okay," I agreed. But I knew that his story wouldn't be that scary. After all . . . he was talking about nightcrawlers.

Worms.

Nothing he was going to tell me was going to make me afraid of worms.

But I was wrong.

When I met Jim on the playground later that day, he told me a story about nightcrawlers that scared me to the bone . . . .

next in the

AMERICAN CHILLERS

SERIES:

#15:

NEBRASKA NIGHTCRAWLERS

continue on to read a few terrifying chapters!

1

"There," I said to myself as I looked at the sign I had just made. *"That'll work perfect."*

Here's what the sign said:

JIM'S NIGHTCRAWLERS
BIGGEST IN TOWN
1 DOZ. = $1.00

As you've probably guessed, that's me: Jim Newkirk. I live near the village of Denton, which is a small town just outside Lincoln, Nebraska. Lincoln is the state capitol, and it's also where I was born. I don't know where *you* are, but where I live, we're surrounded by fields and farms. There's only one other house nearby, and it's across the street. That's where my best friend, Brittany Olson lives.

And you're probably thinking that I make a little extra money selling nightcrawlers.

Not true.

I make a *lot* of extra money selling nightcrawlers. I hunt for them at night, and I sell them to fishermen. This is my third summer selling nightcrawlers. Last year, I made over two hundred dollars! Not bad for a ten-year-old kid in Nebraska. One day, I'd like to open a shop in our garage and sell more than just nightcrawlers. I'd like to sell different fishing lures, and maybe even fishing poles, too.

But right now, nightcrawlers are a big business. The reason? I always seem to find the biggest nightcrawlers, and I have a lot of customers that come back just for that reason. In fact, one of my customers caught the biggest catfish of his life with one of my nightcrawlers!

I picked up the sign, carried it to the front yard, and stood it up in the grass. Then I stepped back.

That will work just fine, I said. *And it will last a lot longer than my old one.*

The last sign had been made out of cardboard. Which worked fine—until it rained. Then it got ruined, and I had to make another one. I found a big piece of wood in the field behind our house, painted it orange, and used black paint for the letters.

Hunting for nightcrawlers is actually kind of fun. It's not always that easy, either. It's best to hunt after a heavy rainstorm, because the ground gets soaked and the nightcrawlers come to the surface to breathe. You have to walk through the grass really quiet and look for them. And you have to be careful not to shine your light right on them, because they'll get scared and go right back into their holes. Plus, once you grab them, you have to be careful not to pull too hard.

All in all, I think I'm pretty good at hunting nightcrawlers.

But things were about to change.

This summer, I was going to discover that while I was hunting for nightcrawlers, nightcrawlers were hunting for me!

It rained all day Saturday. Actually, it started drizzling Friday night, and the rain soaked everything. By Saturday evening there were puddles everywhere, and I knew that it was going to be a great night hunting crawlers. There would be more than I could catch myself, so I put on my raincoat and walked across the street to the Olson's house. Brittany Olson is my age, and she sometimes helps me catch nightcrawlers. I don't know many girls who like to catch crawlers, but I pay Brittany four cents for every one she catches. And I still make a profit when I sell them to fishermen.

I knocked on the door, and Mrs. Olson let me inside. Brittany came out of her bedroom. She was smiling. Her black hair was pulled back in a ponytail.

"I knew you'd be over," she said with a smirk. "It's been raining all day."

I smiled. "Want to make some money?" I asked.

"You bet!" she said. "What time?"

"Meet me in our garage just before dark. And get ready to catch a lot of crawlers!"

Our parents are pretty cool about us staying out after dark when they know we're catching nightcrawlers. After all, it *is* the best time to catch them, so they allow us to stay out really late sometimes . . . as long as we don't go far.

"All right," Brittany said. "See you tonight!"

I turned and left. I was really lucky to have someone like Brittany to help me catch crawlers. She's gotten really good at it, too. She knows how to walk softly, and to be careful with her flashlight so she doesn't scare the them. A lot of girls at school can't stand touching nightcrawlers, but Brittany doesn't care.

Besides, she's making money. Together, we catch twice as many nightcrawlers as I do alone.

Back in the garage, I checked on my inventory of crawlers. I have a special styrofoam box where I keep the crawlers. I make a special bedding for them that keeps them alive for a long time. Actually, the bedding is just old newspapers that I run through my dad's paper shredder. I get it damp and then clump it up. It's not the best bedding, but it's free. I put a little dirt in as well, and I make sure that the inside of the container stays moist.

My nightcrawlers were doing good. I guessed that I probably had a few dozen, but I would need more really soon. Saturdays and Sundays are my busiest days, because those are the days that lots of guys go fishing. Sometimes I have a line of fishermen at my garage, waiting to buy my crawlers.

Just before dark, Brittany met me in the garage. It had stopped raining, and the evening air was warm and damp.

"Hey," she said, as she walked up to the garage. She was carrying her flashlight, but it wasn't on.

"Ready for a night of crawler hunting?" I asked.

"Yeah," she said, turning to look at the soaked grass. "It's going to be a great night for it! I saw your new sign, too. It looks good."

"It'll last longer than those cardboard ones," I said. "What I'd really like is to get one of those blinking signs, but they cost a lot of money."

I handed her a coffee can with a little bedding at the bottom. Then I took off my sneakers and put on my old, grubby work shoes. I've learned not to wear my good shoes when I hunt for nightcrawlers. They get wrecked pretty quick when they're getting wet all the time.

I grabbed a coffee can for myself, and we headed out. We started in our front yard, then moved to the back yard.

Just as we suspected, there were lots of nightcrawlers all over the place. The rain had really saturated the ground, and a lot of worms had come up to get air. In no time at all, Brittany and I each had caught a couple dozen.

Darkness set in, and crickets chirped like a symphony. We turned on our flashlights, making our way into a big field that is behind our house. The field isn't mowed, and there are lots of burrs to watch out for.

But it's the best place for nightcrawler hunting!

Brittany was a couple hundred feet from me. All I could see was her flashlight beam.

"I can't believe how many there are!" she called out to me.

"I'm finding a bunch, too!" I hollered back, just as I spotted another big, fat crawler in the grass. I reached out slowly, grabbed it snugly, and pulled gently. It twisted and squirmed, but it came out of its hole. I dropped it into my coffee can and set out to get the next one.

"I think I've got—" Brittany had started to say.

But she didn't finish her sentence. Instead, she started *screaming*.

I had no idea what had happened, but I knew she was in trouble, and I needed to get there . . . and fast. The only thing I could do was run as fast as I could to help her—and hope that I wouldn't be too late.

"Brittany!" I shouted. *"I'm coming!"*

In the near distance, I could see her flashlight beam pointed at something. Beyond her, I could see the dark shapes of our houses. Lights glowed in the windows.

I kept running. My shoes sloshed through the wet grass. My pant legs beneath my knees were soaked.

"Brittany!" I shouted again. *"Are you all right?!?!"*

"I'm fine!" she shouted back. She sounded angry. "But my brother's not! He's going to be in a lot of trouble!"

I heard snickering and laughter. I slowed as I approached the glowing flashlight beam. She had the

179

light trained on two figures in front of her. I recognized one of the faces right away. It was Brittany's brother, Bradley. He was wearing his bicycle helmet, grinning from ear to ear. In the glow of the light, I could see that he had mud caked all over his face. In one hand he was steadying his mountain bike. As I got closer, I recognized Kevin Miller, a friend of Bradley's He, too, was wearing his helmet and had a mountain bike. Like Bradley, Kevin had mud all over himself, too.

"That was funny!" Bradley was saying. "We were just riding our bikes across the field, and I saw your flashlight. I thought it might be you, so we turned our headlights off and snuck up and scared you!"

"You're a goofball!" Brittany snapped.

"And you're a chicken," Bradley replied sharply.

"Hey, Bradley," Kevin said. "I've got to go. I'll see you tomorrow."

"See ya," Bradley said. Kevin hopped on his bike, turned on the headlight, and rode his mountain bike through the dark field.

"Are you all right?" I asked Brittany again.

"Yeah," she replied. "Bradley and Kevin just scared me, that's all."

"You're afraid of your own shadow," Bradley sneered.

Which really wasn't true at all. I've know Brittany for a long time, and she's not afraid of many things.

"Come on," I said to Brittany. "We've got work to do."

"Hey, I was just leaving, anyway," Bradley said, and he hopped onto his bike, clicked on the headlight, and rode off.

Brittany shook her head. "He's such a dork," she said. "He's always doing things like that."

"Forget about it," I said. "How many nightcrawlers have you caught?"

"I lost count at fifty."

"Wow! We're going to have a ton of them before the night is over! Let's keep going!"

But our hunting was interrupted only minutes after we'd started again.

Our hunting was interrupted by screaming, and we both knew who it was.

Bradley.

And we could tell by his terrible shrieks that he wasn't playing a prank this time.

In the darkness, we couldn't see where Bradley was. The only thing we could do was head in the direction of his screams.

And he was yelling something, too. Saying something about something coming after him. But he was in such a panic that we couldn't understand him.

"That way!" I shouted as we sloshed through the wet grass. I aimed the flashlight in front of me. As I ran, I wondered what could possibly have scared Bradley so badly. He's fourteen . . . four years older than Brittany and me.

We came across his bike, laying sideways in the grass.

But there was no sign of Bradley.

"Bradley!" Brittany shouted. "Where are you?!?!"

"Over here!" Bradley called out, but his voice echoed strangely, like he was up in the air.

How could that be?

In the next moment, we found out. In the middle of the field is a big maple tree, and I shined my light toward it.

"Up here!" Bradley gasped. "But watch out! It'll come after you, too!"

I shined my flashlight up. Sure enough, Bradley was sitting on a branch, high in the tree.

"*What* is going to come after us?" I asked nervously, shining my light around.

"That . . . that . . . *thing!*" he shrieked. "It came after me!"

"What came after you?" I asked again.

"Yeah," Brittany said. "And why are you in that tree?"

"It was a nightcrawler!" Bradley screeched.

I almost started laughing.

"A . . . *what?*" I replied.

"It was a nightcrawler! Honest, it was! It was as big around as a car!"

Now I *did* laugh. That was just too funny!

"How about that?" I chuckled. "Your brother is afraid of worms!"

"It's not just any worm!" Bradley protested. "Honest! It was gigantic! And it came after me!"

Brittany and I shined our lights around the dark field. The only thing we could see was wet grass.

"I think you're imagining things," Brittany said. "There isn't any such thing as giant nightcrawlers. Now . . . come down out of that tree before you fall and break your neck."

It took a few minutes, but Bradley finally came down. He glanced around quickly, his eyes darting everywhere.

"I'm telling you, the thing was a monster," he said. "It was huge!" I thought he was going to cry.

"Oh, for Pete's sake," Brittany said. "You're acting like a baby!"

"Where's my bike?" Bradley asked.

"It's over there," I said, aiming my flashlight beam so he could see his mountain bike. He jogged over to it and stood it up. When he dropped it, the light had gone out. He turned on the headlight and swung his leg over the crossbar.

"I'm getting out of here," he said. "And you guys should, too! That giant worm is still out here somewhere!"

And he took off, this time pedaling like crazy.

I laughed again.

"Can you believe that?!?!" I exclaimed. "A giant nightcrawler!"

"As big around as a car!" Brittany chortled, and we laughed for nearly a minute. We couldn't believe that her older brother had been chased off by a worm.

Soon, however, we wouldn't be laughing.

We wouldn't be laughing at all.

Even though we only had one flashlight, we continued hunting for nightcrawlers. We teamed up, and I would hold the light for a while and Brittany would catch the worms. Then we would trade, and she would be in charge of the flashlight while I snapped up the crawlers.

And man . . . did we score! It turned out to be one of the best nights of crawler hunting ever!

It was getting late, and I was getting tired. Water had soaked through my shoes, and my feet were cold and wet.

"Well, it's been a great night," I said. "I think we caught over ten dozen nightcrawlers!"

"That's awesome!" Brittany said. She was carrying the flashlight. I had just caught my last nightcrawler, and we were going to go home.

"I'll have a busy day tomorrow," I said. "It's supposed to be a nice day. I bet I'll have a lot of customers."

"I ought to set up a lemonade stand across the street," Brittany mused. "You could sell nightcrawlers to the fishermen, and I could sell them lemonade. We'd make a fortune!"

"That's a great idea!" I said. "You should try it."

"I might. I think I'll—"

Brittany stopped speaking. She had her flashlight trained on something up ahead of us.

"What's . . . what's *that?*" she asked quietly.

I peered into the darkness, but I didn't see anything.

"What?" I asked. "What did you see?"

Brittany took a couple of steps forward, then stopped. "There," she said quietly. "Right there."

Ahead of us was a low sloping hill. Not a steep hill at all. Most of the area where we live is pretty flat.

But in the side of the berm ahead of us was a cave-like hole. It was big, too . . . big enough that if I wanted to go inside, I probably could. Oh, I'd have to bend over, but I could go inside.

"That's weird," I said. "It looks like a cave. I've never seen it before."

We watched for a minute.

"Let's go see what it is," Brittany said, and we walked closer. When we were only a few feet in front of it, we stopped.

It was a cave, all right. Or a hole of some sort, dug into the side of the berm. Brittany shined the light into it, and the cave appeared to angle down into the ground and keep going.

"That's really strange," I said. "I've been all over this field, and I've never noticed this before."

"Me neither," Brittany said.

"Want to go exploring?" I asked.

Brittany shook her head. "No," she said. "It doesn't look safe. The last thing we want to happen is for the whole thing to cave in on us."

I hadn't thought of that. It probably isn't a good idea to go exploring giant holes in the earth.

"Let's go home," I said. "We'll come back some time when it's daylight."

We turned to go . . . but we didn't get far.

"Wait!" I whispered. *"Did you hear that?"*

We stopped and turned.

"Yeah," Brittany replied. *"I heard . . . something. From that hole."*

Then we heard it again.

A noise, coming from inside the hole in the berm.

But it was already too late when we discovered that whatever was in the hole—

Was coming out!

We backed up, keeping our flashlights trained inside the strange cave. Roots dangled from the top of the hole.

And suddenly, we could see movement. I froze. Brittany gasped. We both backed up even more, ready to turn and run away.

As it turned out, the creature came at us so fast that we wouldn't have had a chance to run if we tried. I jumped, and Brittany let out a shriek.

Fortunately, what emerged from the cave wasn't a monster . . . but a dog! It looked like it might have been a German shepard, but I couldn't be sure. What I *was* sure of was this:

That dog was *scared*. It ran past us with its tail between its legs. In seconds, it was gone.

"Wow," Brittany gasped. "That thing freaked me out!"

"Me, too," I replied.

We kept our lights trained inside the strange hole. There wasn't really anything to see, but one thing was certain: *something* really frightened that dog.

Finally, I swept my flashlight beam away. "Well," I said, "it was probably scared off by some other animal. Maybe a skunk or something."

I looked up. Stars winked back at me, and a half-moon glowed. The crickets continued their rhythmic chiming.

"It's getting late," Brittany said. "We should probably get home."

We trudged through the field with our coffee cans and our lights. Soon, we were in our garage under the cool glow of white florescent lights. Across the street, a couple of lights were on in Brittany's home.

I set up my table next to Dad's Suburban. On the floor, I have a large styrofoam box where I keep all of my nightcrawlers. I lifted it up and put it on the table.

"How many do you think we got altogether?" Brittany asked.

"Tons!" I replied. "It sure was a great night of crawler hunting!"

I placed an old newspaper on the table and we emptied our coffee cans onto it. Both of us got to work counting our nightcrawlers.

"Sixty-five!" Brittany exclaimed, when she had counted her last crawler.

"Sixty-two!" I said. "You caught three more than I did!"

I kept a small amount of money in a mayonnaise jar on Dad's workbench. I walked over to it and unscrewed the lid.

"Let's see," I said thoughtfully. "Sixty-five worms at four cents each. That would be . . . "

I had to think about it. I'm usually pretty good at math, but I wanted to make sure I gave Brittany the right amount of money.

". . . two dollars and sixty cents," I said after a moment of thought. I dug out two one-dollar bills from the jar, then counted out the change. Then I screwed the lid back onto the jar, placed it back on the workbench, and walked over to Brittany.

"Here you go," I said, handing her the money.

"Thanks," she said, and she took the money and stuffed it into the front pocket of her jeans. "I've got to go," she said. "I'll see you tomorrow. Thanks again for the money."

"Thanks for the hard work," I replied. She turned and jogged home, disappearing into the darkness.

Seconds later, I heard the front door open across the street. Light spilled out, and Brittany's silhouette appeared in the doorway for a moment. Then the door closed behind her.

I put away the big styrofoam box, folded up the table and went inside. Mom was reading a book at the kitchen table, and Dad was watching the news on television. When Mom saw me, she looked up from her book and smiled.

"How did you do?" she asked.

"Awesome!" I replied. "We caught a ton of nightcrawlers!"

"Well, get cleaned up and head off to bed," she said.

Any other time, I would have asked to stay up later. But not tonight. I was tired. I was sure I would fall asleep as soon as my head hit the pillow.

And I did . . . almost.

The last thing I remembered thinking was about that dog. Why had it been so scared?

And Bradley. He claimed that he'd seen a giant worm or something. It sounded crazy . . . but he really had been scared.

But the last thing I remembered before I fell asleep was my decision to hike across the field in the morning to get a better look at the cave . . . or whatever it was.

It would be daylight, and I would be able to see it a lot better.

It was a decision that I would forever regret.

FUN FACTS ABOUT CALIFORNIA:

State Capitol: Sacramento

State fish: Golden Trout

State Nickname: The Golden State

State Song: "I Love You, California"

State Bird: California Valley Quail

State Motto: "Eureka" (I have found it)

State Tree: Redwood

State Insect: California Dog-Face Butterfly

State Flower: California Poppy

State Mammal: Grizzly Bear

Statehood: September 9th, 1850 (31st state)

FAMOUS CALIFORNIANS!

Shirley Temple Black, actress, ambassador

Robert Frost, poet

George Lucas, film maker

Richard M. Nixon, U.S. president

Tiger Woods, golfer

Jeff Gordon, race car driver

Jack London, author

John Steinbeck, author

Joe DiMaggio, baseball player

Robert Redford, actor

among many, many more!

Also by Johnathan Rand:

NOW AVAILABLE! Johnathan Rand's exciting sequel to
'Ghost in the Graveyard':

GHOST 'N THE GRAND

About the author

Johnathan Rand is the author of the best-selling **'Chillers'** series, now with over 1,500,000 copies in print. In addition to the **'Chillers'** series, Rand is also the author of the 'Adventure Club' series, including **'Ghost in the Graveyard' and 'Ghost in the Grand'**, two collections of thrilling, original short stories. When Mr. Rand and his wife are not traveling to schools and book signings, they live in a small town in northern lower Michigan with their three dogs, Abby, Salty, and Lily Munster. He still writes all of his books in the wee hours of the morning, and still submits all manuscripts by mail. He is currently working on more **'American Chillers'** and a new series of audiobooks called **'Creepy Campfire Chillers'**. His popular website features hundreds of photographs, stories, and art work. Visit:

www.americanchillers.com

Don't miss these exciting, action-packed books by Johnathan Rand:

Michigan Chillers:

#1: Mayhem on Mackinac Island
#2: Terror Stalks Traverse City
#3: Poltergeists of Petoskey
#4: Aliens Attack Alpena
#5: Gargoyles of Gaylord
#6: Strange Spirits of St. Ignace
#7: Kreepy Klowns of Kalamazoo
#8: Dinosaurs Destroy Detroit
#9: Sinister Spiders of Saginaw
#10: Mackinaw City Mummies

American Chillers:

#1: The Michigan Mega-Monsters
#2: Ogres of Ohio
#3: Florida Fog Phantoms
#4: New York Ninjas
#5: Terrible Tractors of Texas
#6: Invisible Iguanas of Illinois
#7: Wisconsin Werewolves
#8: Minnesota Mall Mannequins
#9: Iron Insects Invade Indiana
#10: Missouri Madhouse
#11: Poisonous Pythons Paralyze Pennsylvania
#12: Dangerous Dolls of Delaware
#13: Virtual Vampires of Vermont

Adventure Club series:

#1: Ghost in the Graveyard
#2: Ghost in the Grand

www.americanchillers.com

AudioCraft Publishing, Inc.
PO Box 281
Topinabee Island, MI 49791

Join the official

AMERICAN

CHILLERS

FAN CLUB!

Visit www.americanchillers.com for details!

For information on personal appearances, motivational speaking engagements, or book signings, write to:

AudioCraft Publishing, Inc.
PO Box 281
Topinabee Island, MI 49791

or call
(231) 238-0297

About the cover art: This unique cover was designed and created by Michigan artists Darrin Brege and Mark Thompson.

Darrin Brege works as an animator by day, and is now applying his talents on the internet, creating various web sites and flash animations. He attended animation school in southern California in the early nineties, and over the years has created original characters and animations for Warner Bros (Space Jam), for Hasbro (Tonka Joe Multimedia line), Universal Pictures (Bullwinkle and Fractured Fairy Tales CD Roms), and Disney. Besides art, he and his wife Karen are improv performers featured weekly at Mark Ridley's Comedy Castle over the last eight years. Improvisational comedy has provided the groundwork for a successful voice over career as well. Darrin has dozens of characters and impersonations in his portfolio. Darrin and Karen have a son named Mick.

Mark Thompson has been a professional illustrator for 25 years. He has applied his talents with toy companies Hasbro and Mattel, along with creating art for automobile companies. His work has been seen from San Diego Seaworld to Kmart stores, as well as the Detroit Tigers and the renowned 'Screams' ice-cream parlor in Hell, Michigan. Mark currently is designing holiday crafts for a local company, as well as doing website design and digital art from his home studio. He loves sci-fi and monster art, and also collects comics for a hobby. He has two boys of his own, and they're BIG Chiller Fans!

www.americanchillers.com

All AudioCraft books are proudly printed, bound, and manufactured in the United States of America, utilizing American resources, labor, and materials.

USA